25/6/19

KT-559-222

...rd
...od at
...the diocese...ity. She
...the diocese... an Ignatian
...tual director, a therapist a... Duty Chaplain
of Westminster Abbey. *Towards Mellbreak* is
shortlisted for The Writers' Guild Best First Novel
Award and the Edward Stanford Travel Writing
Fiction Award.

MARIE-ELSA BRAGG

Towards
Mellbreak

VINTAGE

1 3 5 7 9 10 8 6 4 2

Vintage
20 Vauxhall Bridge Road,
London SW1V 2SA

Vintage is part of the Penguin Random House group of companies
whose addresses can be found at global.penguinrandomhouse.com

Penguin
Random House
UK

First published in Vintage in 2018
First published in hardback by Chatto & Windus in 2017

penguin.co.uk/vintage

A CIP catalogue record for this book is available from the British Library

ISBN 9781784705015

Printed and bound by Clays Ltd, St Ives Plc

Penguin Random House is committed to a sustainable future
for our business, our readers and our planet. This book is made
from Forest Stewardship Council® certified paper.

For the generations of my family who have
lived quietly on the Cumbrian fells

*But he himself went a day's journey into the
wilderness, and came and sheltered under a juniper tree:
and he requested for himself that he might die; and
said, it is enough; now, O Lord, take away my life;
for I am not better than my fathers. And as he
lay and slept under the juniper tree, behold an angel
touched him, and said unto him, arise and eat.*

1 Kings 19:4-5

Contents

FAMILY TREE of HAROLD

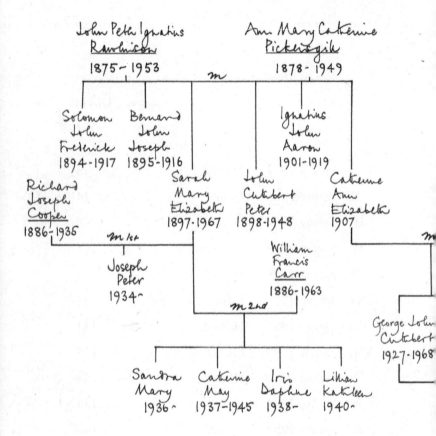

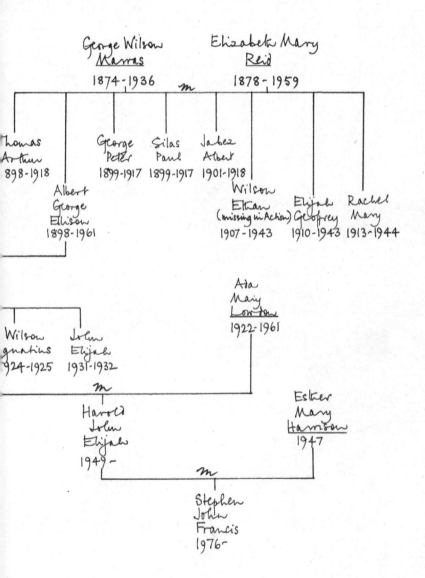

George Wilson
Marras
1874-1936   m   Elizabeth Mary
Reid
1878-1959

Thomas
Arthur
1898-1918

Albert
George
Ellison
1898-1961

George
Peter
1899-1917

Silas
Paul
1899-1917

Jabez
Albert
1901-1918

Wilson
Ethan
(missing in Action)
1907-1943

Elijah
Geoffrey
1910-1943

Rachel
Mary
1913-1944

Wilson
Ignatius
1924-1925

John
Elijah
1931-1932

Ada
Mary
Lawton
1922-1961

m

Harold
John
Elijah
1949-

m   Esther
Mary
Harrison
1947

Stephen
John
Francis
1976-

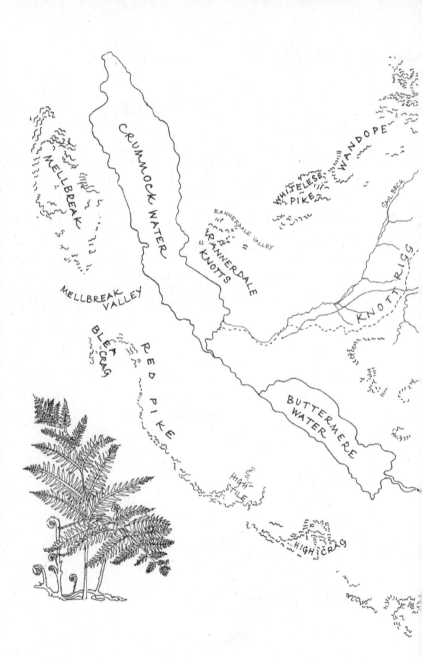

MELLBREAK

CRUMMOCK WATER

RANNERDALE VALLEY

WHITELESS PIKE

WANDOPE

GILL BECK

RANNERDALE KNOTTS

MELLBREAK VALLEY

KNOTT RIGG

BLEA CRAG

RED PIKE

BUTTERMERE WATER

HIGH STILE

HIGH CRAG

SAIL

ARD CRAGS

ARD FARM

NEWLANDS PATH

KESKADALE

BECK

MAP
of the
North-Western Fells
CUMBRIA
Showing some of the
landmarks from
ARD CRAGS to
MELLBREAK

ROBINSON

DALE HEAD

GREAT GABLE

FLEETWITH PIKE

HAYSTACKS

Prologue

Night turned to darkness, the scree a devil's weight on his back. Purple at his side. Shingle fell to a shrill flute, deceitful ground, but he scrambled on, slate unfolding to waterfalls at his heels; it was made to shred him, bleed his arms till they were wet. Dawn on his mind.

Further down, bracken lashed and wrapped him into the banks until the grass left him bare. Heaven a veil of lead. Wind growling. And still, hands dripping, he stumbled to find a march in his stride. Arms spread like a sail, shirt billowing, towards Mellbreak.

I

Spring 1971

Harold

Ard was in its beginning; rock opening its winter cracks to splay sorrel, thistles bulbous and ready to bleed, new grass and nettles creaking under heavy boots. If Harold could feel the rumble of spring, it rose out of the fells today, *almost a stampede in it*, he thought. Bright morning lifting the green so high it was luminous.

He checked along the flanks towards Sail. Sheep were bedded in, suckling the fell like new moss. Down by the beck he turned west, Wandope standing to his right in purple scree, Knott Rigg boned and loyal to his left, Crummock Water ahead, not yet seen but felt, like a promise.

Once he found sheep huddled in that beck. The only time in the twenty-odd years he'd been out with his father. The very part where most water flowed after hard summer rains. It puzzled his father when they came over the fell and saw them; white wool matted together in twos and threes, water pushing at their backs. He remembered his father's face, purple cheeks veined from the bite of high winds; brow no more lined with a frown than without. He said it was as if the sheep were made to be vulnerable. 'Like a magnet they are, to needing care.'

Will, one of his collies, was coming back at a good canter with Toby quietly behind. Harold whistled. Neither of the dogs looped back on itself to show him a find, so he kept walking through the folds of Whiteless Pike, bluebells soon to be spread as thick as bracken, dotterel song at his back, his father alongside him, though he'd been gone for a few years now. And there it was. Crummock Water. A swell to its edge. A silver offering before Mellbreak valley on the other side. Clouds over there often blaze-bellied, breaking for streaks across the twin peaks as if the heavens were in conversation.

Back up the valley, he passed Wandope again, heather ruffling its back as if the rock had just surfaced in budded skin. *For such a dark fell*, he thought, *she's often lit up. Never been mined. But there's a secret in her.* He stopped at the old juniper by his farm, patting its crumpled bark, more of a habit in passing, really. His grandfather Albert proposed to his grandmother under it the day they got the farm. Building not changed much since then: cottage walls still rippled white around its slanted windows; lichen blotting the slate roof. Stone barn crouched to the side like a ewe. There was a new barn in the yard but you couldn't see it from there. The Harrisons would be visiting tomorrow with Esther. *Might be bringing her to the juniper tree one day to bind in a new family. She might be right.* But he wouldn't think of it now, too soon for that. And then he was into the back field, sheep bustling around him, jostling forward for what they thought was an extra feed. 'Damn yows,' he muttered while he dug

4

into the mud to tie the legs of a feeder to a couple of hooks. 'Oor, now git!' he roared and they shuddered back, only to creep in again, hustling into the same climax as before. He finished his knot. The new nylon was good until a frost when it frayed more than the old rope, dried out like an argument, spitting orange instead of burying into the mud and resting with last year's peat. He turned – 'Go on yer scoffs!' – and waited for the sheep to move, their backs bundling into each other, heads above the sea of wool, wide eyes to the side.

One had a stick bound into her, so he grabbed her fleece, pulling her under his legs.

'No lass, not good for you that'n,' he crooned in a low voice, huddling over, pulling the thorny twig from felted wool, feeling her jolt. 'Not a good'un that. Best away.'

He rubbed her sides with his hands as some would towel dry a child. *Yes, they're vulnerable*, he agreed. *Need a firm hold, but they never learn. As soon as you loosen your grip, they've a panicked heartbeat in them. Spring without summer.*

When he got back to the yard the dogs scattered towards stone troughs for a drink. A bucket of old cloths was still soaking by the doorstep, a new strip of cotton nailed high, same nail as last year, rust and weather blotted onto it. Joe's boots were in the hall. Harold put his in the row and looked along to his father's at the top. They were dusty now, not moved for five years. *Keep their shape well, mind.* It was right to have them at the door, but he didn't like the dust.

'Better get till t'feed afore it's gone!' he bellowed through the narrow, whitewashed hall as he walked, woolly socked.

'Aye, better git in quick,' came from the sitting room.

He shuffled around the oval table, tight against the wall. 'Fair do's?' he asked.

'Aye it's getting up all right,' Joe said, buttering his bread.

Corner seat reached, he sighed. 'Old fencing all right on beck side, though?'

'No, it'll be to do mostly 'n' all.'

Harold raised his brow, stretching his legs. He could see the day in Joe. Fresh faced. *Contagious*, he thought, *sprouts in you just from walking in it.*

Catherine came in carrying a stippled black pot of stew, and the men straightened, waiting for the same ladled portions, same grandmotherly motion of her arm since Harold was a lad. And after she'd hung her cloth and settled in her chair, they all tucked in, silently eating till their plates were nearly clear.

'Aye, could feed more lambs onto the fell for the next couple of years if you've a mind to it. Broader flock up there without it tumbling,' Joe said, his bread soaking into the juices.

'She could take it. Blooming mess those registers, though, diven't know who's been grazing what on the fells really.'

'We've all our own way of writing the count!'

'Be right. Wouldn't like to wager how old Jim'd write his!'

'But there's no local differences up here, according the Ministry. All the same culture as some clerk behind a desk down south apparently. They'll find out one way or another. Mind, we didn't include the shearlings or the hogs in ours so we can easily argue a higher count overall. Another thirty-five of each. No harm to the fell.'

'Right, we'll think on it,' Harold said with a deep breath.

'Be tight on the books; we'd need a good winter. So, did you get to the county court this morning?'

'Yes we were there. Made no difference. But they put on a good show when it came to getting the map. You could hear them calling down the corridors, "Call for the map, call for the map" and after a while, two men marched in, one in front of the other with it on their shoulders the size of a rolled carpet! No copy of it, you see. And when they unrolled it onto the floor the QC had Geoffrey walk over and point to say his family had always grazed here. And William do the same.'

'Then what?'

'Well he decided based on what landlord their tenancy was with and said it was more likely that they originally grazed on their landlord's land.'

'So Geoffrey lost the other side of the fell.'

'He did. QC never known a fell more than a visit.'

'Not good news. William's never used it for years. Did you hear anything about Robert's tenancy?'

'Not at the court, no.'

'But from any there?'

'No, it'll be done now. No going back. Landlord will be after a cut of the big farm subsidies and they're not shy of saying they'll get less rent for three small farms than for one big one.'

'Small like ours, you mean!'

'That's it.'

'Marvellous!'

'Truth in jest!'

'Well then.'

'Anyhow, we've not enough lowland here worth changing our farm for.'

'Be about right,' Harold mumbled passing the bread. 'But it's hard to believe Robert couldn't negotiate. Don't know how long they've been there.'

'He'll be a loss.'

'How they renting the farm out then?'

'Off the fells and into the fields for a big dairy herd, maybe a crop or two and fatten more of our fell lambs be the sum of it.'

'They've been here since before the first war.'

'Have that. Know the ways up here better than most. Generations.'

'Not easy,' Harold said, both sitting back, plates empty, falling into silence, the pendulum clip of the grandfather clock warm in its polished wood, Catherine clearing her own plate.

'Off to the shops, Trin?' Harold asked.

'Yes, nothing to add till t'list?'

'No, no, very good.' Harold leant over the loaf to cut another slice. 'Not sure on the price we'll get for store this year.'

'No but the milkers are good and steady.'

'Yes, aye, they're good.'

'We will need a bigger flock on the fell though, bloody Ministry upping the stakes.'

Harold raised his brow in agreement. Joe was right. He was spending more time in the workers' meetings speaking out against the Ministry that regulated their work, pushing up demand and not respecting the culture and traditions of local hill farmers. Sometimes when they talked Harold struggled to find a way forward. Things were getting worse.

The small subsidy they had per head of sheep for working in 'severely disadvantaged' land didn't go far, and after spending the year lambing, dipping, gathering, checking and clipping in all weather, they sold their lambs on to a lowland farm to graze for a few weeks between crop growth, and the lowland farm got double the price for the final lambs. Nearly twice the subsidy of a hill farmer for a few weeks' work. And the lowland farmers didn't depend on the lambs for income. Seemed to be designed to keep demand high and hill farmers poor. *Always need to keep your eye on a new way through. Comes into view when you least expect it.*

Harold took a breath as some would smoke a cigarette and watched Joe mop the gravy left on his plate. The movement helped him rest. More of an uncle than his dad's cousin really, working with them since the second war. Too young to go to the trenches with Harold's father and grandfather Albert. The clock chimed and struck one with the sound of Catherine clattering in the kitchen, her cloth still hanging neatly on the chair. *She's still hand-stitching sections of those old rags*, he thought. *Has her way of things.*

'Fencing this afternoon?' he asked.

'Aye.'

Catherine came back in, buttoning a black woollen coat, her grey hair pulled into a small bun as usual. 'Now, Palm Sunday march after church and then four o'clock tea, Joe. If you're not for the church, it's to be ready for tea, mind. Harrisons will be visiting. You with us, lad?'

'No, Catherine, thank you. I'm off to Lamplugh. Spend a bit of time with our Sandra and the family.'

'Right you are, I'll give you a tin.'

'Lovely, she'll be pleased with that now, kiddies've always room for your cakes!'

She nodded to say a deal had been struck. 'And yours in there,' she said pointing to the metal tin with a portrait of Elizabeth II at her coronation.

'Ginger?' Harold asked hungrily.

A smile flickered across her face as she turned to leave. 'I'll be taking the car now for church-cleaning, mind.'

'OK Trin, no bother,' Harold called as he waited for more instructions to the sound of her walking through the hall, his mind drifting. And for a moment the two men sat in a full-bellied rest. 'Subsidies for drainage is the thing now,' he said, studying the tabletop. *He'll not like the idea of them assessing and advising the farm*, Harold thought. 'Could send a letter, an "application" for to take water off the top of Ard and Sail, drain the marsh areas to get more grass up there.'

'On the fell? They've only diggers! Be clowns to try a digger up there.'

'Mire needs clearing,' Harold said quietly, avoiding Joe's gaze and opening the tin. 'She'd have a fuller pelt if we got the bogs off her.'

'You seen those bloody tractors furrowing up the peat hills? Never!'

'But they'll likely offer, or as they say "allocate", is it?' Harold said, handing the cake over, wide eyed, soon cracking a sly smile, Joe jolting back cutting into a laugh, thumping his fist on the table, 'Aye, let's see them try. Aye lad,' he flared in a deep growl, 'be a good day out watching!' And both leant back, Joe scratching his ear, sniggering, ginger cake in lines of gravy and crumbs on his plate, the distant sound of Catherine driving through the yard.

The next morning, cows milked and sheep checked, Harold was in his only suit waiting by the fire, black coals smoking from the soot of being shovelled on to last the morning. Esther's family would be arriving later. He'd known her since he could remember but not really spent time with her. Hardly spoken in gatherings, nothing more. *Not stood near enough to her for it. Could be a match. Maybe. Would be good to fill out the place.* 'No pressure,' he mumbled confused by the thought of her. Catherine came in, pulling on her gloves.

'You look grand,' she said, her nod emphasised by the small brim of her hat. And with a clip, her handbag shut and hooked over her arm, bible in hand, they stood poised for a moment, as they always did, a familiar respect for the moment before leaving.

Up Newlands path they walked in polished shoes, a slim wind streaking their backs. Tight coils of bracken knotted the banks of rusted stalks, parting occasionally for spliced thick-leaved snowdrops, fierce in their stems. And as the hill steepened, the two of them climbed, gently swaying like rocking chairs past Robinson; their even pace holding its rhythm. After about an hour they rimmed the peak of Newlands path and a small church came into sight in the next valley with a few people walking into the side gate. Catherine watched them, he thought, as if they were words on a page.

When they got to the west entrance a dozen or so stood at the foot of the steps. Jim, an old friend of Albert's was surrounded in conversation, leaning on his stick, medals from two wars hanging in lines. His grandson Isaac quiet at his side.

'Hello Catherine, Harold,' he said, firm grip to his hand. 'Spitting image of your father,' he added looking Harold in the eye. 'Grand fettle was George, he was that.'

Harold chatted, hands in pockets. The sound of Jim had the fullness of his own father and grandfather. When he looked around to find Catherine amongst the people arriving, she'd settled by the wall next to Jim's wife Mary in almost the same black coat and hat.

A bell began to toll and the crowd streamed up the red sandstone steps, and through the wrought iron gate into the church; wooden pews glossed with polish, the heavy hymn books, prayer books and bibles lining their shelves so carefully they looked chiselled in. At the altar, two large palms woven with hazel and silver birch crossed over in an arch, almost hiding the stained glass of Mary and Martha. And the small pipe organ, size enough to surround one man, creaked its stoppers and keys as if the wood were part of its hum. Catherine put her bible on the shelf as they knelt. Harold often felt emptied when he prayed. Words, especially the long prayers, stumbled in him; it seemed enough to kneel, bent in his chest, humbled. The wind sounded stronger inside. *Must be stone bringing out the noise*, he thought. And as the priest read Luke's passion, Catherine's finger lining every word, Harold thought of Christ's walk to Calvary. Grey clouds, lit from beneath drew his sight out of the clear window to his side. They moved slowly towards Haystacks. *Willingly*, he thought, remembering the harsh fells when the tide of winter was up against him. *Can only be done will-ingly or you fall.*

After a while, the prayers were over and they all stood to sing 'All glory, laud and honor,' while David, who farmed the other side of Rannerdale, and his grandson Tom, lifted the large palms from the altar and processed down the aisle with the priest, their grip on the white stems as firm as for any flag. Everyone filed out behind, picking a new cross of knotted silver birch from a basket, singing '*the company of angels are praising Thee on High,*' and once they were down the steps they began the next hymn 'Ride on! Ride on in majesty,' their voices thinning in the air, '*the hosts of angels in the sky look down with sad and wondering eyes to see the approaching sacrifice.*'

Past Bridge Hotel, Harold held back with a group of slower walkers around Jim and Mary; Isaac still at their side. *Skinny lad and as shy as a sparrow*, he thought. Hymns continued to streak through the fields between silences, the sound of Sourmilk waterfall drumming as they neared the lake. And in time, they all gathered along the shore to look out over Buttermere towards Honister Pass; Fleetwith Pike leaning into the water before the wind flecked its reflections like a fleece. David and Tom walked to the shore and waded in, suited with wellies, which made Harold smile, and they ceremoniously set the palms so their stems were just walking on the water. Young Tom looked like he was holding his breath in concentration, small ripples widening from his feet, while they formed an arch to the east. And once it was clear they

13

had set the mast, everyone sang 'All People that on Earth do Dwell,' their voices held together by the valley, '*O enter then his gates with praise.*' Harold watched the trembling arch. Its leaves crossed in the wind. And when he peered through, beyond the low crags of Robinson, he saw the high peak of Dale Head towering in bare rock.

Later that afternoon Harold's hands were so washed they were ruddy red, his hair combed to the side, clean trousers, shirt and jumper. He didn't like the feeling of soap, it stripped the day off him. Everything around his chair by the fire was awkwardly in line, Catherine weaving to and from the kitchen, head down, her small wrists reaching through buttoned cuffs as she laid out cakes and sandwiches. The carpet over the stone floor had been cleaned so hard he could see red thread from the frayed edges.

'You'll not sit there when they come,' Catherine said.

'No.' He leant forward, not knowing where to go.

'We'll give them the chairs by the fire.'

'Aye.' He stood up and looked around the room, not finding an easy alternative.

'Well maybe at the table in the corner, then they'll have more choice.'

'Aye. More choice.' And he sidestepped round the table, shuffling bent kneed onto the chair by the curtains in the corner. Catherine came back in with her pinny off and a flower brooch on her blouse, her light blue sleeves so straight they must have been starched. Harold was glad he had a jumper on.

'Oh,' she said, a small shake of her head. 'You look

14

too far away. Maybe best you are in your old seat. More homely.'

Deep breath, he pushed the chair out to a clank on the wall and started back.

'But you'll stand when they come in so they have a choice.'

'Aye, a choice.'

Once the Harrisons arrived, Harold hovered by the mantelpiece taking in the scent of cedar logs, especially chosen for the occasion. The smell seemed to anchor him when visitors came, but he felt awkward at the sight of Esther. Perched on the edge of his chair, he held a china plate of cake on his knee with one hand, saucer with a cup of tea in the other, mindful of the clean carpet. He was hungry, especially for bilberry sponge and cream, so once Mr Harrison put his cup and saucer on the carpet, Harold did the same and tucked in. When conversation started, he realised that he and Mr Harrison were facing the hearth and had to look to the side to see Esther and her mother. His father would have moved his chair with a joke and made them all laugh.

'You've a good bilberry cake,' Mr Harrison said, looking over to a small nod from Catherine. 'Well now, Harold, how's the flock?' he asked, gently leaning back in his chair.

'Very good, very good.' He knew his face was red from not knowing how to look at Esther.

'Been a few times up there with your father. Seems only a few year back now. It's a fair ground up there.'

'Aye.'

'Changes everywhere though.'

'Aye.' Harold struggled.

'Still a good spot, mind.'

'Oh aye, it is that.'

'One for a tale was George, I'll give him that!' Mr Harrison leant to his side. 'I've not forgot the cobalt mines after his stories of the use of them. And he could talk about Egypt! Quiet otherwise, mind. No small talk in him, but he had his ideas about things.'

Harold smiled.

'Got that in you too, eh?'

'Aye, well, not so much.' Harold blushed again.

'Had he travelled?' asked Esther sitting neatly next to her mother, both in chairs brought round from the table.

'No he didn't, no. Except for the war of course. He did Burma then for a while. Asked for it. But once he was home, no. Stayed put, likely. His uncle John travelled,' Harold said, looking to his grandmother for clarity.

'Yes, John did the travelling.'

'And Albert in Burma as well?'

'No, he was in a base in York and then Hampshire. Worked the storeroom.'

'No easy job those days. You in the fields?'

'We were.'

Harold looked at his cup searching for a new subject.

'A keen reader, though, George,' Mr Harrison added in soft admiration.

'Was that,' said Harold.

'Do you still have his books?' Esther asked.

'Yes, shelves of them. Good insulation,' he joked with an open smile.

'That what your mother, Ada, called them?' Mr Harrison joined in.

'Yes.' Harold laughed. 'No, well, she liked them,' he said, squeezing his legs from the awkwardness of bringing truth into a joke. 'They would do it together when she was here.'

'Reading?'

'Aye, of an evening, with maps.' Harold edged his chair away from the fire a little to face the others.

'John – that the eldest brother of yours, Catherine?' Mr Harrison asked.

'No, Solomon was the eldest. John came fourth out of six.'

'Stayed there?'

'Cholera,' she said in a slightly high voice. Harold looked down at his tea; he could feel Esther watching him.

'Missionary, wasn't it?'

'Yes, after the war. First war.'

'Bring it out of him likely, did it?'

'Always in him really, always thinking on religious things.'

'Aye,' he said, turning his head in thought. 'Brave man to be doing that now, after those times. Kept the faith. Brave.'

'They brought back his bible,' Catherine said, looking towards the cabinet next to the hearth, 'and his stole.'

'Well now, that's good of them to do that. Long way Egypt with the desert n'all,' he said, breathing out, letting the dust settle. 'Long journey that one.'

'China, it was China where he worked.'

'China he was?'

She nodded.

'Oh, now I'm not sure why I thought it were Egypt. Sorry. Did he ever get till Egypt?'

'Just at the end after the war for a while, but his work was in China.'

'China,' Mr Harrison repeated, looking into the fire for a while. Catherine offered Mrs Harrison another scone and Esther sat quietly, broad flowers on her skirt, sipping tea.

'Did they ever meet up out there?' Mr Harrison asked without turning. 'George being close enough. Burma road. Did he meet with John? Be a shame to miss the chance so far out there?'

'Not that we know of.'

'Didn't talk much about it.'

'No, but after the war, we got a package of letters John couldn't send.'

'All in one go?'

'Yes, he'd saved them. Couldn't get them to George at the time, you see. Well, he got one or two to him, but it was good to have them all.'

'It would be. Nothing like a letter.'

'True,' Catherine said a light shake to her head. 'Not easy beat was our John. And George often read them,' she said looking to Harold.

'Did that,' Harold nodded.

'Yes, it was maps in the evenings,' said Catherine, 'and Ada liked to paint. Watercolours. That's one of hers there,' she said, looking above the fireplace. 'Crummock Water.'

'Oh, it's lovely, Catherine, Harold,' said Mr Harrison, looking up.

'She liked lakes.'

'I've looked at that a few times here and bless me I never knew it was hers,' he said twisting to see it in full view. 'Twin peaks of Blea Crag and Mellbreak fell in the back if I'm not mistaken,' he turned, looking for confirmation. 'Lovely woman your mother. We all felt the loss of her.'

Harold kept his eyes on the painting and then the harvest barley plait around an apple hanging to its side.

Quietly Mr Harrison added 'And Albert, Catherine, sorry.' He shuffled awkwardly. 'Never pass Bringley Road without thinking of them. Never easy,' he said, one hand holding his wrist. 'Seems some days are put here to show us it's never easy.'

'Lovely colours,' said Esther. She was looking up at the painting, wide blue eyes. She glanced at Harold and smiled. He wasn't sure if he smiled back, but he gazed for a moment. There was something peaceful about her. He flickered his sight to notice her broad calves stretched out, ankles neatly crossed, and then her face again, oval cheeks. She was taking in the painting, almost dreaming, while Catherine started talking to her mother about their distant cousins. There was something about watching, her look. *Tender cheeks*, he thought. And he noticed that she held her saucer with an outstretched hand, fingers closed, like a leaf.

In the evening he went up to check the sheep again, a little weary from the day, a scuffle of last winter's leaves matted into new grass. He walked over to Sail and settled with his back to the old cobalt mine, watching the valley. Good to have a bit of time to himself. The sky rumbled low in charcoal grey, a slit of light prising open the horizon. Old

Robinson in shadowed bow looked chained to the green-stone of Great Gable beyond. He could feel his father sitting with him, painful at first, but he could almost see him, pale faced after a full day. Muddied black boots out front, quietly steadying himself for another tale of those mines. Stories brought rest into him, binding worries with pigment to yield blue glass bottles for perfumes sold across trade routes, necklaces in manor houses, paint to capture the sky, Chinese pots, Egyptian scarabs and falcons hidden in buried tombs. Tales, which could only be told sitting there. 'Come on, marra,' he'd say when Harold was barely five, 'we'll gan and see what's happening to t'Emperor.' And once he'd turned and tipped his cap to Sail, round and solid behind them, he would lean back, his gentle voice full of ardour, song-like, sometimes no more than ten minutes, other times into the night, following smugglers, trackers, travellers and sculptors into a tale. Better than comics. And on evenings, after a silent slump watching buzzards circling the thermals, swifts darting, he might turn the birds into messengers, wearied journeymen not always reaching their end, their bravery rarely known but sometimes carved into statues of turquoise and gold.

'Should that one be carved, Dad?'

'Aye lad, he had a fair shot at it, dues given.'

When Harold was twelve, after his mother and grandfather died in the accident, he and his father would stay up there late into the night. The two of them peering over a new book of constellations in torchlight. Orange glow from Keswick far off to the east, to the side of their view, almost holding their grief in its light. A manageable distance, a warm companion not forgotten. His father began to remember 't'olden days'. Memories often repeated but enjoyed again. 'Thou's great gran'd be up here of an evening, picking some root or other, she'd say with the moon or heavens. Knew about the life of things. She called that'un' – he pointed to a constellation – "T'old Chalice". Where "the sight" comes spilling out onto them that has it. Tears of Christ she would call it. Tears from heaven giving the sight. Thou diven't wish on that'un. Not always a barry guest, that.' But if rain or clouds drained the glow from Keswick, they packed up without asking, not because a storm might follow the valley towards them, but without the glow, it seemed their grief was frighteningly close. His father pale, almost childlike as they walked home. Sadness so far into his father's chest, it emptied him and drew Harold tight to his side, marching together. But it was never long before they'd find Catherine waiting for them by the juniper tree or in the porch. A warm tumbler of milk to take to bed.

Harold thought about the afternoon. 'Fine lass,' he heard his father say, and remembered her blue eyes looking at the painting, and her skin. 'Thou thinks as I do son, but diven't give breath till it.' Harold knew he wouldn't be like his father, following maps and reading into the evenings with his wife. Ada had been around the farm as an extra hand for milking, butter-churning and hay-time before the war. Stayed on through it. She'd known George when they were young, maybe even watched over him as she was five years older. After the war, she was one of the few able to talk with him. It took a couple of years of his silence and Catherine's help, but she

21

found a way. She was like that; patient to find a way. But it was different times for Harold. When he planned a family he had to be practical and realistic. He had what he was given in life and he was more independent than his father. He needed to build the farm up to keep what they had. Pass something on to his children and grandchildren. See them planted about the fells. *Beware*, he thought. *Spread too far and you lose your grip. Too little and you gain nothing.* He shuffled back against some old planks, muddied black boots crossed out front, arms folded and stared ahead. *If hard work has anything to do with it I'll have something worth giving. Not easy beat.* He remembered Esther in the sitting room and felt rested. *Might be a fit*, he thought. *Find evenings of our own. She would take that sewing work in. Embroidery in the evenings. That would be different, something new. Could be a little like Mother's painting with the colour of things.* He sat with the silence for a while, wind clearing his mind. *She might be content with what we have. It isn't the life she's known, but it's something.*

Before he turned in for the night Harold got a call from Jake, a friend working in Ireland. He'd been raised on a farm near Skiddaw, always a bet on to beat his time for shearing. 'Fine time to be calling, Harold, but I've given yer a ring, as we've got the scab again down here. Diven't know if it's over yon way, but thought 'twould be good te tell yer.'

'Oh,' Harold dropped his head. 'I'm sorry to hear that, Jake. Have yer got it bad?'

'Aye. We think the lot'll have te gan. Nut sure yet, but. Aye it's a sour lot to see them all scragged out like that. A sour lot.'

'Not bloody right. Poor beasts.'

'Aye.'

They were silent for a moment, then, flushed with regret, Harold said, 'And you'll be all right for work Jake, will yer? There's a place here if you're thinking on it.'

'No, no, I'll be staying to see it through is all, and then, well. Aye.'

'Here if you need it.' He waited.

'Aye. Right ho.'

'No bother, thanks, Jake.'

Harold put the phone down and sat quietly in his chair. He could see the sheep with their wool lumped and trailing, skin blotched, cracked, their legs giving way. He'd known the occasional one sectioned off in auctions, but a whole flock would be something else. He wanted to go into the fells again and check. *No sign of scab in them*, he thought. He'd given them a thick coat of Diazinon after shearing. Longthwaite's were using the new chemical stuff, but it was expensive and no one said it worked any better. They were taking it off the shelves in town, Tyler said. So, well, he'd have to keep an eye out for it at the auctions. He could feel their fleece bulging in his arms. Their softness given over for spindling into winter warmth. A vulnerable gift.

Through the night the wind was up with such a force that what was often a gentle moan around the windows turned into a melodious holler. In the early hours he looked out. The clouds hung low. Trees lit in shadowed sleep. His back prickled with cold. He dropped the curtain and got back into bed, wrapping in to reheat the sheets. He would sleep a few more hours and check the sheep before light.

II

Autumn 1973

Esther

Her mother handed over the brown paper shopping list and went outside to wait. Bell clanging over the door. Esther stood in the store. The walls concertinaed with shelves of new cans; their keys hanging to the side next to the usual dangling twists of mop heads, plastic packets of coloured clothes pegs, string, boxes of buttons or metal coat hooks. She methodically worked through the list, gathering things onto the counter one by one, regularly checking her mother's straight back through the window.

'Needing a rest is she?' said Morris, waiting behind the counter.

'She gets confused.'

'Aye, not an easy one.'

Esther smiled, steadied by the rhythm of gathering things onto the counter while he noted them down with his pencil.

'Your Shirley well?'

'Yes, aye, she'll be here after the bakery as usual.'

'It was a lovely job they did with those harvest festival plaits this year. All that decorating.'

'She's good with that kind of thing. I'll just go and see if your mother—' Morris walked outside to the sound of the bell again and Esther watched her mother turn, say something, then shuffle to the side. Then, they both stood, backs to the window, Morris's blue overall ruffled from his hands in his pockets, watching the street. When Esther finished going through the list, everything neatly arranged on the counter, she sat on the stool Morris had brought around and waited a while, sweet smell of dust and varnish, wondering what look her mother would have if she turned to peer through the window. *The questioning would be too much for her now. Squinting into a dark place to find something,* she thought. *Knows the street at least; old waiting place. If she did turn to look through the window, her face would be younger. Probably impatient with a list of things to do! She wouldn't turn now.*

Morris came back in and added everything up on his notepad, his stained fingers careful with the pencil. He wrapped the leeks in brown paper, 'good crop Willy Roberts has this year,' and pressed the long black till buttons for the final amount.

'Thank you, Morris,' Esther said looking to the window again.

'Nae bother, lass. We'll look after them yet.'

'Aye, she just needs settled. Likes the old memories best.'

'We all do!'

'Ready now,' Esther called brushing her mother's side, tartan bags in hand, stopping for a moment to swing into step together, her mother following behind at an uneven pace.

Her slim-fingered gloves hanging to the sides of her coat, never reaching for the pockets.

They waited at the bus stop in silence. The road was busy today. Her mother didn't like the movement.

'Use the handles, Mother,' she said as they got on the bus, and once they were in their seats she offered a handkerchief and sticky toffee, both taken and held, the toffee then taken back and unwrapped.

'There you go now,' she said, her gaze trailing out to oak trees deepening in heavy red.

The bus dropped them fifteen minutes from the Manor gates and they slipped through the side entrance, always finding a rhythm back in the gated ground, Esther's mother now at her side, beech trees dipping their amber branches in drizzle, leaves glazed in thin yellow. *Like an aisle of stained-glass windows,* Esther thought, enjoying the image when it came every autumn.

Further along, the path opened to a lawn, drawing Esther's sight into gaps between leather green rhododendrons, a never-ending maze of grass and bush. Soft places to play when she was a child, if work was done. Remembered more these days, almost nostalgic. *Leave home and I turn into an old woman,* she thought. And as the path bent, turning away from the Manor, she leant to see the fountain of Neptune with his chiselled beard and broad chest calling to his nymphs and the straight lined pillars around the front entrance.

'Fountain's not on, Mam. Mr Briggs still hasn't unblocked that water, he'll not be in a good mood today! Dad'll be roped into it, likely.'

By the time they arrived at the row of five cottages, her mother was ahead, impatient for the key. And she led through the sitting room into the back kitchen to immediately roll up her sleeves at the sink.

'Take your coat off, Mother,' Esther said as matter-of-factly as she could, unpacking things into their usual place.

Her mother looked down with a tut, as if seeing someone else in their coat, and struggled again to turn up her sleeves. Esther stopped unpacking and stood next to her, there was nothing in the sink to clean, but she'd soon bring things from the cupboards. She looked out of the window to the yard, knowing her consistent gaze might take her mother's eyes out there and make space for a new thought. The washing line was waiting to be filled, small red brick washhouse to the side. The gate to their narrow allotment was scoured with leaves. Westmorland damsons hard knotted along thin branches.

'Mam, can I have that pinny you've on to wash now? We're doing a turn and it needs freshening.'

'No, no, I'm all right now, love,' she said, looking out with Esther.

'Damsons will be ripe soon.'

'Good, about time.'

'We've not got one load on the line yet and they'll be asking for them at the Manor,' Esther said and though the words came from years ago, the phrase made her mother's arms hover for a moment and obediently peel off her coat, struggling with furled sleeves, and then, fresh pinny on, she grabbed the dish soap, turned on the taps and ruffled the water to a light haze of milk.

Later they went through the yard and sat in the old wash-room, cup of tea in hand, biscuit tucked into the saucer.

Empty wicker baskets laid out neatly in a row across the long table and all three paddle machines gleamed from being wiped down.

'Sarah and George Wiggins have had a baby, Mam,' Esther said with the pleasure of good news.

'Have they?'

'Aye, a little boy.'

'Oh lovely, boys sleep more than girls.'

Esther smiled. 'Well now, guess what they called him. Three guesses.'

Her mother gazed to the ceiling for a moment. 'Um, John.'

'No,' she said, thick tea sweetening her throat.

'Geoffrey?'

'No,' Esther said slowly to keep the excitement.

'Not George,' she said her face crumbling into a giggle.

'Aye, it'll be young George, father George and grandfather George. Can you imagine around mealtimes . . . can you pass the salt, George!'

They laughed, the idea of the new baby so familiar to her mother, she enjoyed the surprise every time, tutting in the same place, 'poor loul thing!'

She was almost her old self, surrounded by years of long days starching and folding. This small washroom wasn't used for the Manor now. The new machines were in a bigger outhouse but Esther kept the room clean for them to sit in. Her grandmother's chair still to the side. She could imagine her there, always in her black dress and pinny, a handkerchief in the cupped pocket. When Esther was small she sat on a stool next to her learning how to stitch, despite her broad hands. Cross, plain, double looped. 'Strong fingers,' her grandmother would say every now and then, feet planted in her old slippers, thick tights crinkled at her ankles. And if light from the small high window was bad that day, she might say 'Better than in the fields,' perhaps remembering the rains that had weakened her Fred's chest when she'd taken him with her working the farms. Her baby swaddled in the grasses. She always blamed that for his TB after the war.

They talked and then sat a while, Esther's mother murmuring as the windows darkened and the fluorescent light yellowed. Esther wondered what Harold would be doing at the farm. He was a shy man, brusque sometimes but worked hard. A gentle soul, she thought. It had taken him some time to begin courting; and even then he was quiet, waiting. When he proposed under the juniper tree, he'd had his words ready. Almost practical. 'It's a good farm and I've a mind to build it up. Do well for a wife. Not easy is farming, but it's a good life,' he'd said. 'If you'll have it.' Pooled brown eyes staring once he finally looked up. She'd felt them slot into the fell together.

The three of them, Harold, Catherine and Joe, would be having a quick supper and then Harold would read by the fire. There was no doubt she was nervous to be going home tonight to his sitting room again. It was so new. And the spare room to sleep in, cleared out for her while she settled in before the wedding. 'Your embroidery and any other things would be welcome in the evenings,' he'd said a few times, which made her feel uncomfortable. Or 'you can turn in when you like, we don't hold on ceremony here.' When she'd recovered from the spotlight, she found it amusing to think he had

29

rehearsed the lines and given them almost like verse. But she did feel guilty leaving her mother. And more guilty that she felt free to build a new life, new memories, a new home. Harold's parents seemed to have had a good marriage, if the stories of their evenings together were anything to go by. Once Esther was settled, she'd think of ways to fill the farm with colour. Maybe even start painting like Harold's mother, or thread a tapestry for the sitting room.

She patted her thighs. 'Come on then, we'll need to stoke up the fire for Dad coming in,' and she walked towards her mother, anticipating sharp elbows not wanting to leave. 'We'll see if Mr Briggs got that fountain fixed or not!' she added cheerfully. And up they shuffled out into the yard with the usual swaying, as if for a moment her mother lost her sight in the drizzle and wind, steadying through the kitchen into the sitting room and her soft old chair by the fire.

'Doing another pillow, Mam. Foxgloves this time,' she said between blowing under the coals to get a good fire going.

'Why not the linen squares?' her mother called out as if it were a bid in a room full of people.

'You know why,' she said with a tired smile, sitting back. 'I like it.'

'It's not right.'

'What's not right, Mam? It's different, that's all. Nothing wrong with them.'

Her mother shook her head, bottom lip curled into her mouth.

'You make no sense sometimes, Mam,' Esther sighed, regretting her words as soon as she heard them, feeling weary for a moment, then pulling her bag to her chair, refreshed by the sight of coloured threads neatly curled under the cotton. 'Would you like to look at the *Cumberland News*?' Her mother drew her hands to her knees obediently waiting. Esther rustled in her bag again and unfolded it onto her lap. 'Wonder who's getting married then?' she said settling into her embroidery, wind fluting the chimney. 'Another spring scene, but this time I'll be trying foxgloves round the edge. Should be nice, what do you think?' she said holding it up.

'Couldn't sleep on it.'

'They do in the Manor.'

'They say they do,' she mumbled.

'They do, Mam, and it's lovely.' Her mother looked pale and smaller in this room, even her skin was thin as if the veins were calling out in blue to make up for the lack of colour.

'Are your feet sore? Would you like me to rub the ointment in?' Esther asked to a short grimace of disdain as a reply. Her mother licking her fingers to turn the pages, grumpy now, stopping for a moment to read. Esther stitched the points of her foxgloves, a low rain tapping the window. 'Any news, Mam?' she asked, but there was no answer, print absorbing her like moonlight.

The silk thread was fine, as was the needle to carefully layer the small raised buds and petals. She'd spent the last week at the farm with thick needles and wool sewing patches onto the behinds of sheep too young to lamb before the rams were let loose! 'Bratting' they'd called it. The Herdwicks' fleece was so thick it wasn't as hard to stitch them on as she'd thought. Though it was strange seeing them bounce

31

off up the lane decorated with squares of colour. The farm had so many unexpected sights. Even the hayloft changed shape with the coming and going of rectangular bales. Like a collage. A few weeks before, when she'd arrived, Catherine had shown her the layout of the larder with such detail that she'd wanted to take notes. She tried to go through it in her mind but couldn't. The larder here at home was curtained with flowers hanging under shelves and hooks in the ceiling. Her grandmother had dried almost every flower she found, making displays and Esther liked to do the same. It was stocked with similar pickles and jams, but not as many as Catherine's. And they'd never been practical enough to use labels, though Catherine's looped handwriting was difficult to read and often stained. It had been over a month and she didn't like to ask.

That night she got back to her room, which looked out over the back towards Ard. An arched clock ticked loudly on the dark dresser. A family of boys, she'd thought when she was first shown in, though Catherine had clearly put a floral spread on her bed for comfort and they must have wallpapered the room for her, as the bulged circles were fresh and white. After a couple of weeks she'd put the spread of paddle brushes for clothes, shoes and hair that were on the dresser into the top drawer, one by one, keeping the white cotton lace mat. In their place was her embroidery along with a china bell, some dried pink roses and a photo of her parents' wedding, but she still felt clumsy in the room somehow, as if its history padded it out. What little else she had would come after the wedding in December. But in the wardrobe the beginning of her wedding dress hung waiting.

So far, it was only a throw of white cotton nested with tightly wound coloured threads ready to be woven together when she had a secret hour here and there in an afternoon's work. Or time in an evening when she could go to bed early without offending to spread it over her bed and chalk the pattern of stem and bloom to be followed.

In the mornings she was up as early as for the Manor, though it seemed darker out here, the feeling of night in the bedroom even with the light on. She was getting used to Harold being out in the fields before she was in the kitchen, Joe meeting him on his way up from his cottage on the other side of Causey Pike, young collie Ellie at his heels. Every morning they walked the cows in for milking, though just open the gate and they would have made their own way. But there was something about Harold heading out and starting the day no matter what weather, Catherine and her swiftly laying everything for breakfast, a bare-knuckle chill to their pace.

This morning, she checked the dough early so Catherine would see she was getting the hang of the routine and moved it away from the warm night ashes for the fire to be made. The sound of hooves clattered into the yard as regular as a bell, drawing Esther out to the porch, wiping her hands on her pinny. She liked the sight of it, Joe and Harold plodding unnoticeably close to the cows giving their wide backs the odd pat or yelp.

Back in the kitchen Catherine had finished her peeling for the day's stew and started chopping Esther's stack of vegetables.

'They're in for milking now,' Esther said, blushing because

33

Catherine would know from the sound passing in the yard, starting the countdown for cooking the sausages and then the eggs. She went through to the sitting room and knelt to prepare the fire.

'Eh, I'll be doing that.' Harold's voice came behind her.

'I don't mind it,' she said looking up to him, feeling as vulnerable as her first day at school.

'Aye, but it's for me to do now,' he said, kneeling down beside her, carefully taking the shovel out of her hand, his grip felt on hers for a moment and scoured under the grate with a loud shunt, pulling thick ash out and into the ash-box. He looked awkward, knees in line with the fire, but leaning away from her, off-balance. *It's the gentleness in him.* His wrist showed every time he leant forward: ruddy-pink skin with fine, brown hairs.

As he went to stand, so did she, Joe coming in from the hall. 'Morning, Missus,' he said.

She smiled and mimed a disapproving look, 'Morning, Joe,' she said. He liked to tease her before the big day. Harold hadn't moved from in front of her. 'Better get back to Catherine, then,' she said. *His first day at school, too.*

After they'd eaten, Harold and Joe went back to work as swiftly as they'd come. Once the women had cleared, Catherine began her new jars of pickled carrot and beetroot for a church stall. Pearl barley stew sizzled through its slanted lid on a low heat, the pot full now with extra cabbage, offal and jelly stock. Esther went into the yard to feed the cockerel and hens. She felt heavy thighed in her welly boots. Over the last few days Harold had taken time in the mornings to check the tractor engine or sort out something in the hayloft, peering round as she talked to the hens kindly and then couldn't help but give a good stamp trying to stop them pecking at each other, fighting for grain. She could hear him laugh sometimes, and when they flapped back in for grain again, squawking on top of each other, their chests bare to the peck, she would squeal under her breath, darting back, flinging feed into the distance.

Most evenings Joe left after a six o'clock supper with the sound of whistling through the hall. Harold joined him for a final check of the fells and was back an hour later when they would sit, three chairs by the fire. Esther with her needlework or magazine, Harold reading his *Farmers Weekly* and Catherine trying her new glasses with *Reader's Digest*, soon off for an early night. 'Like to sleep when it's dark,' she'd say.

At seven Esther phoned to check on her mother and whoever was with her, but the only phone was in the sitting room, and her calls got shorter. 'Hello Mam, it's me, you had a good day?' After a while, when she was cleaning, Esther placed a vase of dried flowers to the side of the hearth. Aware of it in the evenings, sometimes a colourful contribution, other times a jug with no scent by the black iron grate. One evening Harold asked if she liked it, if she liked the farm. 'Yes,' she replied, surprised by the question. 'Very different from our back garden!' she said with a laugh.

He smiled at the fire sizzling on young oak ripe with sap. 'It'll be that all right!'

And then, Friday came around again, helping her mother on the bus. Good for her to go shopping, though it made her nervous. And home through the gates, along the beech path, washing the old machines down, an easy sandwich supper with tea waiting for her father who took most meals at the Manor now. Tuesday and Friday afternoons were all Esther had there, and Sundays. Catherine went to church with Harold if his chores were set. Joe had Sundays off, though he was often found sorting something on the farm in the afternoon, and Esther left early. Her mother had stopped going to church years ago. 'Too much work on,' she would say, and Esther sometimes helped with the Sunday school or embroidered a kneeler for Easter. But as the illness spread through her mother's memory, it was as if they had always gone, and so, neatly dressed, they would get a lift at the gates and stay for milky tea in the hall, Sunday lunch cooking slowly in the oven at home. Food served, her father would say 'Nothing I like more than Sunday lunch,' like a prayer before they started and he would give Esther the news from the Manor. 'New maid settling in, never be as good as our Esther, but a nice lass anyhow,' he'd say.

'And the garden, Dad?'

'Dahlias come up lovely this year.' She missed his easy chatter and going outside to see what he was doing, searching for him in the Manor gardens or knowing he was digging his allotment at the top of their long narrow garden before he went back to work. Her cakes baking, soon to be brought out to him still warm.

*

A month later, the wedding was weeks away, though it felt much nearer and Esther was spending more time in her bedroom working on her dress. The air was warm between her and Harold. She was getting used to his habits. In the evening, when he first sat on his chair, knees wide to the fire, he would be still for a moment absorbing the heat, before he picked up something to read. He liked to sit at the table after a meal with an empty plate in front of him, restless if the plate was taken away too soon. And he couldn't hold a conversation in a corridor, it would make him frustrated, edging into a room to ask you to say it again. They didn't speak much, but she was aware of sinking deeper into herself when she sat near him. And that when he was out of sight, he pulled her axis like a sail.

One afternoon he asked her to walk up the side lane with him towards Ard. She set well with his pace, though she would have been nothing like his speed if they had been on the steep sides of the fell. Not far up the lane he opened a small gate into a patch of ground behind the farm, overlooked by three oak trees, their leaves caught in the tops of tall grasses, nesting in. White meadowsweet was thick along one side, mauve valerian surfaced, tall and skinny, and towards the back, by the bushes, a long feathered patch of yellow iris stalks waited for next spring. Her grandmother would have slipped them into an arrangement; drying them in the larder.

'It's a grand spot here,' he said.

'It's lovely,' she whispered, light rain spotting her cheeks.

'Well, it's yours for the taking if you want it.' She looked at him, his brown eyes seemed vulnerable. 'Aye, if you want it.' She let her gaze sweep over the ground again, breathing in the smell of it. 'Like your garden at home. Well, it could be if you had a mind to it.' She looked up, wordless. 'Well then, that's settled,' he said. 'We've been wanting some good lines of carrots and potatoes on the farm again.'

'Potatoes?' She looked at him, startled.

'Aye, be good to have them.'

She looked over the meadow, questioning.

'Well, I don't suppose we'd have to,' he said, waiting. 'Maybe just a little patch, eh?' She nodded, not to appear ungrateful.

As he turned to leave she said, 'A lovely place to sit, Harold. Some flowers about.'

'Oh,' he said, looking around as if there would be evidence of their mark somewhere. 'Runner beans make a nice flower.'

'They do,' she said, amused at this choice.

His smile widened, broad, and crooked. 'When you mentioned your garden at home, I thought it might do.'

'It does.'

'Well then,' he nodded as if they were in the auctions and a deal was done. 'Good,' he said as he walked off towards the gate.

She turned and watched him go, giving a small wave when he looked back before the gate, and then she lifted her sight to the sky without the cobbles and concrete, stone troughs and metal machines. Lifted her eyes through the oak trees to the breadth of clouds and wind, resting, finally resting in a place which could be hers, if a few rows of potatoes were given over.

What was that? It fleeted through. And again – what was it? Gone in the bushes by the back wall. Now it pushed through, opening the leaves without making a hole, standing stretched on its hind legs, long grey-brown ears, its black

38

eye, waiting. She didn't move, hardly breathed. *Is she a mother?* she wondered. Then the doe bent, chestnut fur opening to the ground like a rocking chair and chattered over the grasses, stopping for a moment to look up, jet eye, and then to the grasses chattering again, her furred neck gently bobbing like silk.

The next morning Esther came up to the meadow in the morning after feeding the hens and cleaning, and the next at the same time with the doe in mind, hoping to see her again. She planned the flowers, noting what was there, thinking of the cuttings she could get from the Manor, and made sketches to garden all but a wild section at the back under the oaks, which she would leave quiet and untouched in hidden vetch for the doe, except for adding a few wild flowers like foxgloves, ragged robin and chamomile next to the iris and large ground elder. But the bushes the doe had come through would be untouched, leaving her scent. And she planned to corner off a strip along the far side for a few vegetables, which she would hide behind plants, still keeping a good shape for the garden. Oh, a flash of brown fur crackled through the bushes and gone again. Esther stood still, waiting to see if she would come back. Wall-barley blew into curves, its fringe softening the breeze. *If Grandma had been given a garden of her own would she have filled it with wild flowers from their walks or ones from the Manor?* After a while a raven creaked over the sky, its sound making the fells seem distant. It circled, flew towards the farm and over the buildings above the yard, croaking again against the stone. As she left she looked back at the three large oaks now almost bare

39

leaning over the far part of the garden. *Autumn passes faster up here*, she thought. One branch had kept some of its leaves.

Back inside, late morning, she lifted the cloth from the dough. It had risen well so she kneaded it for the second time, warm and firm in her hands, almost human. Catherine had gone to visit her cousin for a few days leaving Esther and Harold in the farm together. She managed the chores but pottered and contemplated in a way she couldn't normally; Catherine was so fast and detailed. For a moment the sun streaked lines on the bank of grass outside the window. Tufts lined the slope as if they were waiting to roll down. And beyond, out of sight, was her garden. She wiped a plate dry in circles. She was settling in, but sometimes, she did feel large and in the way, though Catherine never said anything. *Wouldn't it be lovely*, she thought, *to put a box of flowers and herbs along the window ledge. Rosemary would grow well with little light. I'll have to ask Catherine. No, maybe wait a while for that.* And suddenly she missed the high windows of the washroom at home, or the kitchen window, clothes on the line, her father somewhere beyond the gate. It all stood in her body like a bruise. *The memories will leave me tired.*

That afternoon, Joe and Harold rumbled down the hall in heated banter towards Esther's ginger biscuits, still a little warm, and large chunks of fruitcake.

'Might have to chain them together to stop them!'

'Horn to horn.'

'Good cake, Missus,' Joe said, awkwardly reaching around

the small vase of flowers for a slice. She gave the honorary shake of her head and poured the tea slowly, thinking it might settle them.

'He's talking about the new ram,' Harold said with a smile. 'Likes to wrestle with the others.'

'Lads together, and it's to be in that pen for a year before it stands proud at the Spring fair. Show a good wintering before we hand him back.'

'Might have to separate them.'

'Strong horns those,' Esther added.

'Wouldn't be behind them!' Joe laughed, though something seemed to be on his mind.

'More?' Esther asked, holding up the teapot to them both nodding. Joe took a deep breath, 'one bad winter ... we'll have to think of something.' Harold looked down without answering. 'Their progress, our risk. Even if you're up for the change, it's too fast. Blind. Be contracts for clipping next, no more evening's crack with everyone around one of Catherine's fine spreads,' he added, restlessly lumping rhubarb jam onto his cake. 'Do it their way and we'll lose our selves to depend on. Institutionalised, that's what we'll be. Dangerous. It was all right to get help during the war, we were one man depending on the other – oh, pardon Missus, no bother meant.' Esther shrugged and tried to smile. 'But they've no community in them now, just politics.'

Harold didn't move and quietly muttered 'We've no choice, Joe.'

'Maybe, but it'll be a hard lot without milkers.'

'Without milkers?' Esther asked.

'Yes, well, aye,' Harold turned with a look to the side as

if the news had been given too soon. 'The dairy's gone on to better things than our old milk churns.'

'Better things!' Joe repeated.

'It'll be better for them, likely.'

'Better for who is the question.'

'So what will we do with the churns?' Esther asked.

'No, well, they've moved on to the big tanker trucks, you see. And we've neither the equipment nor the farm fit for it.'

'You mean there's nowhere for the churns?'

'Afraid so.'

'What would we need for the tankers then?'

'Well, on top of the equipment for pumping, we'd have to change the building for their pumps to hook in and we'd have to knock out the yard wall just to get the tankers in.'

'Don't even know if they'd get round the corners on our narrow lanes,' Joe added. 'And they'll only collect every two days and expect a lot more milk. They're made for the big farms. And we'd have to pay.'

'More than for the churns?'

'From nothing to a good price is the difference,' Joe said with disdain. 'Dairy paid for churns, but we'd have to pay for tankers. They'll have been offered some grant or other. Control, that's the Ministry's way. Break up communities depending on each other and drop you as soon as it fits.'

'They might be trying to help with subsidies,' Harold said with a slight smile to Esther. 'Better than rationing and we've paid tax for long enough.'

'Could we keep a couple?'

'Well, not unless you'd like to hand-milk twice a day!'

'Ah,' she stopped, wondering about the practicality of it.

42

'Oh, I wouldn't,' Harold said, apologising for giving her the choice. 'It's not worth it.'

'Bloody golden handshake,' Joe said in a low voice, though he could have been bellowing with the strength in it.

'No.' Harold looked ashamed for a moment and Esther felt still, waiting for things to become clear.

'Well, you see the Ministry's tried to help,' Harold said as Joe leant back. 'They've offered a "golden handshake" to compensate by buying our milkers for slaughter.'

'Smaller fee for slaughter 'n' all.'

'Yes aye, smaller fee in a normal market. At any rate, we're not slaughtering those milkers. Been with us for years.'

'So, we'll practically give them away as milkers with no compensation whatsoever – nothing but loss.'

'But why?'

'Because everyone will be doing it – flood the market.'

'Some small farms will accept slaughter, but most will have had their herd for too long.'

'Is there nothing we could do?'

'No,' Joe said shaking his head. 'Heartless buggers. Grants and guidelines are their stock. Like to see them live with a herd for years. Anyway they'll have worked it out, sadly. Canny way of filling the new big farms with milkers for practically nothing. Making their own landscape.'

'Well, they're not going for slaughter so that's the end of it.'

They stopped for a moment, an air of exhaustion around the table. Harold looked thin.

'And I know you're not happy with the police checks on the dip, Joe, but nobody is. We've just got to get on with it.'

'Police?' Esther said.

'Yes, aye, they've made this dieldrin dip compulsory and it will be to check now, just to make sure.'

'When did you find that out?'

'Meeting last night.'

'Seems a bit much.'

'It is. Police or Ministry men. Be so we all do the same, likely,' Harold said, fiddling with his knife.

'Only have to pass by that stuff and you're dosed!' Joe added.

'Aye but if the flock were overcome by lice or scab, it doesn't bear thinking on, Joe.'

'Don't reckon on it, lad,' he said in a rumbling tone. 'Scab's come and gone for years. It's the carting everything around and their regulations that mix it up. Anyhow, checking up on us ... there's not many'll put up with that. They want to own us, the buggers, they want it all. Sorry missus.' They stopped as if in shock, hardly a breath taken. 'And another thing,' Joe continued, 'them chemicals – mark my words, it'll be some deal or other. Some profit with the companies, likely. That new phosphate dip costs more and we're the fools paying. And no mistake, what they say about them birds of prey having lost eggs because of that other chlorine dip. Never made with nature in mind, only money. If we let it go without a stand we'll be as bad as that lad who walked past the beggar. Bad Samaritan. Strength in numbers. Only way.'

'Aye, but we'll be good at working it out,' Harold said with a weight Esther hadn't heard before. 'Be no room for improvement if we're stuck on nostalgia about t'olden days. An hour a sheep, parting the wool for to butter and tar their skin. Or leather aprons, and those rubber waterproofs our grandfathers had to wear for the arsenic. There's research,' he said nodding to Esther. 'Better than before. It's a new way and there's truth in that.'

They sat for a while as if the news had been spread on the table in place of food. Joe watching in silent conversation. Harold looking down, she thought, ashamed from talking straight to Joe.

'We'll work it out.'

'Aye, we will, somehow.'

Esther and Harold were on their own for supper that evening. They sat for a while by the fire, *Farmers Weekly* unread, watching the flames.

'Things all right with Joe?'

'Aye, frightened of the changes,' he murmured quietly, looking into the fire. 'He'll be right, likely.'

'Means well.'

'Oh aye, he's a good lad Joe, don't get much better.'

She waited a moment, but he said no more, so she read by his side, feeling the pressure in him, wondering if she should ask again. The clock chimed a half hour.

'Ready for supper?'

'Oh, whenever you're ready,' he replied, straightening up as if he felt he should be doing something.

'Well, I'll let you know.'

'Right ho,' he said, taking the paper in hand straighter than usual to read the front page. As she turned out of her chair to leave she felt wide hipped and pleased the paper was blocking his sight. When she came back through the hall later, carrying a large hot casserole, he was in a clean shirt and jumper, wet hair combed to the side.

Standing at the table, she dug the ladle in to get chunks of meat, surprised by how much more aware of herself she was when they were alone, and suddenly felt too big. When she sat, her buttocks spread over the edges of her chair like thick buttered bread. He looked down and she didn't blame him. Her throat was so dry she had to chew small bits, practically suckling them to swallow, cutlery clanging and scraping more than usual. He blushed when he used his bread to soak up the sauce and for his final slice he used his knife and fork like she did, sweeping the plate. She hadn't realised that Catherine being around took so much pressure off. When she brought out a special pudding, even that seemed too much. A raspberry jam sponge with cream meringue, bulging white, seeping into pink. He ate it, pushing his spoon in for another fill and she decided the sweetness would lift their spirits; the table looking different with it sliced and opened in the centre. Back in the kitchen, she washed the plates, hot water on her hands, and dried everything shiny and in its place, while he was in his chair, keeping part of her by the fire. Floor mopped and lights out she went back through, creaking the chair as she sat, waking him from a snooze.

About a week later she was in the yard checking for eggs. Harold and Joe were out somewhere in the fields. A low orange-grey cloud lit up the side of the house making the uneven mortar look pebbled. It spread over the fields like candles. She stared into it, lifting her cheeks and noticed trails of smoke stretching over the slate roof. Panicked, she ran into the house ready for flames burning into the kitchen, but it was coming from behind the farm. Up the hill, the smoke blackened unnaturally thick, as she strode, panting into the scent of nutty seasoned peat, a loud crack, and in the middle of her garden was Harold. He looked up, squinting, a broad smile on his face, pleased to have been discovered, swinging his spade, heaving piles of leaves, stacked high, heavy in slices of layered soggy taupe, hissing puddles of smoke into the flames.

She tripped on the muddied earth. The gate had been taken off its hinges, wooden poles removed to let the tractor in. And she stood like a child left on a city street, smoke streaking into her, then funnelled away by the wind, crackle and snap of sap getting louder, small embers lifting and threading into dust.

'Aye,' he said loudly. 'Thought you were spending a bit more time in here, so it needed clearing.'

She winced a smile.

He smiled back, red cheeked, and leant on his spade for a moment, looking around as if she would sweep a view of the ground with him; drips of sweat on the sides of his brow. Then he bent again, digging. She stepped out of the line of smoke, wobbling on the ploughed lumps, the unearthed blanket of summer which had spread, holding the heat in for winter, the burrows of squirrel nuts, the tips of grass scented from deer and doe, her doe in the long grasses with winter berries and mosses, wood sorrel and anemone, the bulbs, the bulbs for spring, the bluebell bulbs. And all this was his gift, digging it up. His surprise.

47

Three ravens landed one after another on the nearest oak. For a moment their wings were still spread. She looked at the charred rows of soil. *He doesn't know what he's done,* she thought, *means well,* though the sight of it soaked into her. She needed the gates of the Manor as much as her mother sometimes. The long pathway arched with trees between them and the world. *No grass, no cover. Left bare, dug out, exposed.* She looked back at Harold digging in the centre of the garden. He stopped to wipe his eyes watering from the smoke. Her grandmother would say, 'It's no good mithering about it now. Best say to yourself "ash is good for roses", or "a rose is for courage". Plant them in the centre.' The ravens stayed motionless in the branches. *Fearless birds. The robins are smoked out, but the ravens come to watch.*

That night Harold walked down the corridor after she'd come out of the bathroom and kissed her. A neat crisp kiss on the lips and smiled into her eyes. Then he walked back to his room, a firm tread, closing the door without looking back. She lay under the swirls of wallpaper, feeling the space outside her window, the wind sweeping towards her garden. The presence of it used to help her rest, dream, lean out into the night, but now it was as if parts of her body had been rearranged and she slept sweaty-browed, folded into the blankets, her back to the window, eyes so shut they knotted into the past, unfurling gardens, faces, conversations.

III

Spring 1976

Harold

Harold stepped into the yard. It was hard to recognise for a moment, not the feeling of home he remembered when he was young, his parents filling the rooms. Seemed it would be natural for life to feel like those days, their presence with him again, new baby bringing them all together. But he was the parent now, and he brimmed with it, cobbles like proud lumps under his feet, grey sky pressed with light from below, curved like rubber, stretched just a bit bigger. *Clean up the farm and thrive*, he thought. *That's what we'll do. Show this lad how it's done.*

He went back upstairs and opened the door. Esther was pale, almost a red outline to her face. She leant over the baby, smiling, its small gaze already known to her, already close. Catherine next to them, cotton towel in hand. Harold stood carefully, as if he held a candle. A turn of face, a small gesture and the sight of them was painfully disarming. *Better call more of the cousins and let them know*, he thought, and then Esther lifted the baby, his head falling, the shawl around him loosening. His small body wriggling for a moment, face reddened, wrinkling with a whimper while she unravelled the sheets, lifting her nightie, his mouth opening, searching for her, soon suckling and Harold was undone; her softness and the boy's tiny hand on her breast. He had nothing left but to sit quietly and watch.

'Thou's brimming ower!' Joe laughed.

'No denying,' Harold smiled, shaking his head as he pulled over the metal bars for the walkway towards the dip for the next day.

'Be a bugle call any minute!'

'Hey, I'll not be shied by you!'

'Oh, but the little lad'd shy you.'

'He would that,' he admitted to Joe's laughing, testing the pressure for the sheep to push against.

'Golden fleece, that lad.'

'And better.' He didn't quite know what Joe meant, but it was something to do with privilege and the little lad was worth more than he could give.

'Pass this lot on to him and see what he cleaves till.'

'Aye,' Harold said with the strain of stacking bales in to secure the bends.

'End up a mechanic, likely!'

'City lad!'

'Full of new ideas.'

'With the new tractor on its way, he'll not be pulling the old hay scaler welded to a shaft at the back!'

'We'll find another use for it! And will you go for Stanley's herd?'

'As you say, there won't be another flock for sale with

grazing rights on the fells next to us for a long time, so I think we will, Joe. We'll get on with it!'

'Be shining the cobbles next!' Joe laughed and Harold turned to see Esther had come out to the porch with Stephen just a few days old now. And she held him facing out, legs dangling, bouncing, showing him the yard, talking as if his small ears could understand, arms stretching. She waved his hand to Harold.

'Not waving there now, Harold?'

'Nae bother,' Harold growled, tapping the air.

The following morning he woke feeling the night had been another day, with Stephen up again. 'You rest' or 'you've the farm tomorrow,' Esther kept saying as she got out of bed, the sound of crying making him helpless. He'd never realised his heart could peel away so quickly. But this time Harold woke to the memory of the old hut his father did up when he was about eight. They'd passed it abandoned on the other side of Sail for years and then his father just took it over. No harm done. Couldn't remember the last time he was there.

Once they'd finished dipping the last of the hogs, it was well into the afternoon and while Joe took them back up Ard, Harold headed over Sail and into the woods. It was good to be on his own, the path soft in mud puddles from last year's leaves. Thin ash like pewter on either side with pines and beech, their branches stitched with buds. The old hut could be heard in the distance, or that's what they used to say when he was a lad as the stream skewed and lipped in front; sound soon disclosing corrugated walls, the wooden front of the hut barely seen. Close up, the ribbed sides peeled red lead and were sprayed with white powder from moss that had dripped over the tin roof for years. *Still solid enough*, he thought, though the roof was heavy with thatch, a rubble of twigs caught as ground above ground. He checked inside through the broken window, no, the ceiling hadn't a hole or bowed plank in it.

The wooden front still had a brush of blue. He remembered his father painting it with that tin he got as an exchange for something. Now lime green had seeped up, splintering the planks at their base, drawing soil with them. And above the door 'Seldom Inn' was carved into a piece of wood – with whose penknife was it, now? The question taking Harold, for a moment, into scattered footsteps of lads darting around, smoking and playing cards.

He went round to the stream and washed his face in a small spill where leaves and twigs caught in stones like netting, whitening the water as it splayed. His head was heavy, almost flu-like. *Have to get used to less sleep.* The fresh water cooled his scoured hands, unusually raw after dipping. 'Soon gone and job done,' he chanted under his breath to bide the time when he felt bad. It's what his dad would have done to push through a bad back, 'Easy forgotten'.

The door of the hut had to be kicked open. Inside the old bales of hay were grey and muddied. *They'd flake apart given the chance*, he thought. He tapped the old card table, its veneer rotted deep into a black ring, *good line of cigarettes would be there for a bet*. The nails from the frame of the two front windows were easy to pull out, a few shards of glass gathered from the floor. *No, the truth is it's not open to strangers any more. Landowners would want rent for the use of it.* And he

52

wondered how he might give the sense of freedom in the fells to his son now the farming rules and ownership had taken hold as if they designed the land. *Might work it out and get a rental of it or something. Few years to sort it through yet.*

'Good lad,' Harold said out loud, turning towards the bales, as Joe or his father, George, would have said to him when he was young, sitting with them all, smoking. 'Good lad,' he muttered, imagining his son sitting there in a few years as if nothing had changed. But it had. *Prisoners were made to build it and now the local lads are barred from it,* he thought. *Something's awry.* And he set to, chiselling his son's name near his father's, cutting into the damp wood, pleased Stephen would be alongside theirs even if he never played there as vines and lichen grew around their bales, their table, their times and winter snows weighed in, froze and melted. 'We're not beat yet.'

That evening he was late back to a table laid with soup, cake-bread, cheese and a couple of jars of Catherine's pickles. Esther came down part way through the meal, having just got Stephen to sleep again. She looked tired, which seemed to bring out a quiet voice in him. Even Joe didn't say much and ate more than usual.

'Joe says you've been at the old hut,' Catherine said, poised on her chair.

Harold looked to Joe. He didn't remember mentioning it till he came in. There hadn't been time for Joe to tell Catherine.

'What's the hut?' Esther asked.

'Oh, it's where the lads would go; up to no good!'

'Nothing wrong with a few cards and a bottle of home brew!' said Joe.

'Summat wrong with that home brew,' Harold laughed.

'Albert would say it was made by captives in the war,' Catherine said.

Esther smiled, 'Do you think it really was?'

'Could be.'

'Good story, though,' Joe said, his mouth full, stopping to look at Catherine. 'Plenty of places built by prisoners in those days, mind.'

'Aye,' said Harold, noticing Esther wasn't eating much.

'You at the meeting tonight, Harold?' Joe asked, his voice sounding loud compared to the others.

Harold looked at Esther and she seemed nervous but nodded.

'Sure now?' he asked.

'We need to keep up with what's happening,' she said while Joe pulled out his chair.

'OK now, see you in t'yard. I'm off for a smoke. Another magnificent spread, Catherine,' he called in the hall on his way out, Esther closing her eyes to sink back in her chair.

'He'll get used till it,' Harold said, realising that Joe's voice might have woken Stephen.

'I'm all right really, Harold. He'll settle soon enough,' she said, the sound of Stephen coming again from upstairs. 'Go on, and I'll see you later.'

They got to the church hall, a familiar bare rectangle with rows of chairs soon scattered as people came in and found a place to doze or chat. A low rumble of dialect got stronger as the older generation arrived and the younger ones enjoyed the crack. Old Raffers found a place at the back, knees out, leaning forward on his stick. Jim in his large coat over his farm clothes quietly waited in the corner with his grandson Isaac. David and his son next to him. The speaker arrived late, placed a screen tripod in front of the warped portrait of Elizabeth II and, thin-fingered, fiddled with his slides.

'Diven't ken what he needs them for anyways,' Joe said while slide by slide clicked round a circle and onto the screen. 'You'd think we'd not seen a field.'

When the slide check had finished, someone muttered 'We'll be off, then, now that's done!' Laughter ruffling their seats and then an old voice boomed from the back, 'Let's git al' Robert t'come and play t'pianner for t'young lad!' which brought a roar into the room.

'Poor bugger, how do you start after that?' whispered Harold.

'Young Ike'll not ken what's hit him with this lot if there's questions,' Joe said. 'Hardly a whisker on him.'

The lecture began with maps and a diagram, the young man's accent clipping the walls like a foreign flute. The slides showed farmers planting trees and soon turned to a section of field with wild flowers when someone called out 'Whose pile of scrag is that, then?'

'Ministry sheep wanting to pick flowers!' called another through the din of laughter.

'Thou diven't ken which flowers are where, lad,' someone said. 'We've none of them on our fell tops. But we've others. What say your blooming case history about that?'

'Aye, nothing personal, lad,' someone added, 'but we've

55

never all of that lot. There's not the daylight for it on our side, never will.'

The young man stood, waiting.

'Thou've nae chance with these al gadges, lad. Just keep in thou's stride,' Jim boomed from the corner to more laughter. 'Aye keep thou's stride,' others joined, 'take nae heed o'them!' The young man struggling to continue, the room rooting for him, head down over his script of seedings and pollinations calculated until he finished the 'case history for your interest'. Subsidies were then turned to for sheep, drainage, fencing, buildings and lime-spreading. 'About time we had some real talk,' someone muttered. 'You've nothing to say for the hill farms except flowers, but you'll not listen,' said another. And the final information given was about the regulation on dipping with organophosphate. A point by point detailed description of the method and necessity of keeping a sheep under for a full minute and the possibility of being penalised if it was less than a minute, even by a few seconds; the room becoming cold with coughs. And after the new paperwork for dips was explained, the young man handed around pamphlets outlining police checks to hard chairs in defiant silence.

As they left, pamphlets in hand, Harold passed Jim and Isaac who stood tall at his side. 'You'd think we'd been in court with all that,' Jim muttered.

'You wouldn't want his job.'

'Not sure what his job is!'

'That'd be right. How's Mary?'

'Oh aye, good. Not sure what till make of all this, though,' Jim said, looking down. 'Inspections'll be . . .'

'It'll be more paperwork, likely.'

'That it will.'

'You taking to the farm well?' Harold asked Isaac, who gave a small nod in reply. 'Be new ways now to take on for your grandfather,' Harold said, feeling a loneliness in their world.

Isaac looked to Jim.

'New aye,' Jim said. 'He's the one taking on the dipping and all the paperwork. More than I could. Wouldn't say I'm that sure on the wisdom of it. Heard of a lad being timed with a stopwatch, and a 52 second dip with one sheep bolting about had to be done again for another full minute. Like being back in the army.'

'They can change all they like but we'll not see the likes of Raffers tending flowers in a field with his sheep no matter what the "case history"!'

'Nae, lad,' Jim chuckled. 'We'll not see the likes of that!'

The next afternoon the winds were so low they slid over the fells, while the sheep huddled in gullies, lying in wait. Some had strayed towards Crummock Water and needed to be herded back again. Heavy grey reached through the valley with a line of light sleeking through in the direction of Mellbreak. A walk to the lake and back always cleared the weight off his shoulders, shook him out, tired as he was from the sleepless nights, even though it was Esther who got up to go to the lad. Sometimes she brought him into the bed between them, little legs kicking for a feed. *Couldn't sleep with him there. Scared of rolling onto him.* His neck felt tight, almost bolted, and his chest was clogged. *Must have slept in a scrow.*

'Better in a few months,' he mumbled under the wind, leaning into it now as mist stole Sail and the end of Ard, a chilled air racing towards him before streaks of rain hissed.

Catherine had given him a letter that morning. 'We're proud of you, lad,' she'd said, handing it to him. 'With young Stephen. It's not the same as your father having words, or your grandfather, but John's family and that's something.' He'd not opened it yet: wrapped in brown paper. From what she'd said it would be one of the old letters from China. *Best leave it with his bible by the fire till I'm ready. Read it when the squall quietens.* His father had a box of John's letters from the war. He'd read them so often they buried the box with him. It would be good to hear something like that again.

Harold squinted through the rain spittling on his forehead, eyes watering as he heard Toby bark and turned to see the small figure of Joe through the mist walking up from Crummock Water, a sheep around his shoulders, hooves clamped in his hands. He shook his head. Joe could look biblical sometimes, never changing his ways. *It'll have got frightened by the wind and given Toby a hard time, probably a bad leg, maybe broken,* he thought, watching Joe's broad strides, like his father's, breaking into the fell. *Father would have had a song in him though.* Harold could almost hear it. And, face dripping, he stood in wait, hands in pockets, shoulders braced to the rattle of downpour, muttering a verse so close to his breath it spat into the water, not knowing the words here and there.

'Shame on me. Should know the words,' he blew as if the tumble of rocks to the side were scolding him.

*

Back at the farm in the evening he went upstairs where Esther was lying on the bed with her sewing, Stephen asleep down the corridor with the doors open.

'All well?' he asked in a low voice, careful of the way he sat on the bed near her.

'For now,' she said, pushing him forward to fluff up his pillow, her nightie opening slightly.

'Catherine gave me this earlier,' he said, handing her the letter, but she didn't take it.

'I expect it's for you, love.'

'Aye, well, I thought we could read it together.'

'If you're sure. Everything OK with the day?' she asked.

'Oh aye, well, I may have found a deal for Stanley's flock over Rannerdale. It's a chance won't come along often.'

'Good to get the next fell.'

'Yes but it's the flock, they're well hefted.'

'What do you mean?'

'Well you could lease the land but put a new flock on it and they'll try to get home.'

'Get home?'

'Yes, aye. Wherever they're hefted becomes home. There are stories of a line of sheep swimming across rivers to get back home. The flock will have sometimes been there longer than the farmer; passed on.'

'They've more to them than you think!'

'Determined, that's for sure.'

'Can we afford it?'

'Well it'll be pulling the belt in for a while and a lot more work. We can't afford to take another on but we'll get help clipping, maybe even dipping, so . . .'

59

'We'll get there,' she said calmly.

Harold looked at her; there was something peaceful about her leaning on the pillow. 'Thought I might do the feeding in the morning till you're both settled,' he said.

'What feeding?'

'Hens and all.'

'I can manage a bit of feeding. I'm not ill, just tired.'

He waited. It was confusing sometimes. He meant one thing and it came out the opposite. She carried on threading. She'd been doing that next to him for a few years now, settling the sitting room, stitch by stitch, but here in their small bedroom it was too much, material and wool spread on the bed, frayed and bulging with colour. *When they say a young family fills your cup, they're not wrong*, he thought. *Overflows*. And he unfolded the brown paper to find the thin rustling letter, turned to ask if she'd like him to read it out loud, but silently read on:

Central China
Longtan Medical Centre
11th November 1927

Dear Catherine,

May God bless you and draw you to Himself. The Lord must be smiling, as am I, to hear you and the child are well. Albert will indeed be proud. Your news has taken a few months to reach us here and brings joy in hard times. The thought of our young George John starting his life carrying the name which I, our father and grandfather have had the honour to live with in these troublesome and happy lives of ours, will keep me going in the long days. They say the soul lives in the middle of us, and so I pray the name John will bless him and bind the faith and strength of John the Baptist into him. May he cry, 'Make straight the way of the Lord,' forever reminded to keep Christ in the very centre of him. And I, as his proud uncle, will keep him in the centre of my prayers. We are in a chain, Catherine. A blessed one from the first Adam to the last, held together by voice, by name, by actions and of course infused with a grace that cleaves to our souls and joins our faith. I give thanks for the new link of our little George John. One more generation in the line of Christ, and a beloved one at that.

After such news, it troubles me to send you a report, but I am aware it will be expected. Tension is building with the Landowners as the Nationalists advance from the south. We have been told that foreigners need to be vigilant and we hear tales of Buddhist temples being ransacked and statues broken. But refuge is not yet an invisible friend. None of us are sure of what news is getting to England, but your letter arriving here in the mountains has given us hope that those in the cities are in better communication, though we have just heard that the fighting has worsened. The schools and hospitals with foreign workers are finding it unsettling. Sadly, there have been some fires and deaths reported under the accusation of 'Imperialist supporters', but I have no details to send. The mountains we reside in are safer, though still a target for bandits searching for food and what little else they find. Recently we gave refuge to an old woman and her granddaughter who were attacked on the road returning from market. Both had traditionally bound feet and were forced to unbind them by a group of men who also cut their long hair. The old lady's feet were broken. She brought their severed plaits with her and held them as close to her heart as we would a cross. They gave us news of buildings in other mountain ranges that have been burned down.

These times, however, bring inspiration with them and we have just had news that Mr Booth from the Wesleyan medical mission in Han secured a truce from the Nationalists for three hours in his bid to rescue 80 blind and 150 wounded from their compound. Now there's a man with the fire of the Lord in his belly. Patients lined the banks in wait, but the steamer wasn't allowed into the Han river because the Revolutionists feared a ruse and would not allow it to pass. Mr Booth however, having foreseen the need for both tenacity and provisions, lay in wait with his patients for three days, until another steamer was allowed to pass and all given leave to board. A tale to be remembered in such times.

As you mentioned in your last letter, it had indeed been in my imaginings that Our Lord's mission here would be a long way from the war we knew so well. They say what you most fear finds you and He continues to test my strength as I am now forced to remember skills and camaraderie from a time which continues to

haunt. I am ashamed to admit there are days when I
see more chaos than a divine plan and wonder what
direction we are all moving in. Only Our Lord knows
the wisdom of such a cross and . . .

'Did you say there was a problem with clipping?'

Harold looked up. He could feel the swell in his eyes. Catherine had read these letters to him, or some of them, when he was a boy, his parents sitting with them sometimes. To read this now after all this time was – well, it made sense of things. He should never have stopped reading them. Seemed too painful after his father died, but that was not reason enough. *Didn't notice life lacked clarity till now. No point in losing the good old things to clear space for the new.* He needed both. That was freedom: to keep hold of the good and push forward, fire in his belly. He looked at Esther, bewildered for a moment. 'Problem?'

'Yes, Harold, the clipping,' she said, a little impatient.

'Sorry love, the clipping? Was there a problem?'

She rested her tapestry on her lap and looked at him. 'You said you might need help.'

'Oh yes, we'll need to get help with the clipping.'

'Aye, you said.'

'Oh.' He looked around the room, thinking of John in his mountains. The story was in the air. *Vivid, that's the word. Must look at those old books of China again. And the maps.*

'Will you be getting the New Zealanders in?' Esther asked.

And his attention cut back to her again, room changing, the spread of mountain air hanging. 'Yes, might have to as there's not many neighbours that visit for the day any more, old milking stools lined out waiting,' he said, smiling. 'And a good spread for their trouble!'

'Be happy to make the spread,' she said, pulling her tapestry.

'No, most farmers have the machines now or they use the contractors. So if we don't do it for them, we can't ask them to come here.'

'Well, the New Zealand lads get it done quickly at least.'

'True, and it would give us more time to get on with the other chores. I'll talk it through with Joe and we'll find the solution, likely.'

He settled back onto the pillow and felt surprised by a sudden ache that he needed to look after her and the lad. Couldn't lose them somehow. Couldn't leave them with nothing to depend on. He was spending more than he was getting to build the herd next year and keep Joe, couldn't do it without Joe. *Slow but sure. Keeps them all strong if you're strong. Steady as she goes. Not afraid of hard work.* He leant his head back on the wall and thought of John. *Frame the day with a good plan, one step at a time.* And for a moment he noticed the sweet, clean smell of their son around them, and read on.

IV

Spring 1979

Catherine

Catherine sat in the garden, John's old bible on her lap, wiping her hands on her pinny before she read. The morning was white-grey with no sign of clouds. Chores were done for now, flatbread, cake and stock, ready for the next few days. She'd been sitting in this same spot for years, ever since her Albert built the wall. Changing the land from a fellside reaching towards Ard to a small field. For a moment she could see Albert, with his long ginger moustache, shirt buttoned over a yellowed vest, dry-stone walling with William, or was it George? Yes, George and his brother, what was his name now? Harry, poor lad. Never right after the war. Bad eyes and weak. TB got him just before the second war started.

When Albert came home from the war, he was still strong, though it had nothing to do with his broad frame. He said luck was buried out there and that hard work kept you going but didn't save you. Yes, he was strong but the trenches were in him. Never talked about them and she never asked; it would have been cruel to ask him to remember something like that. But there had been moments when keeping the land clear and tidy was haunting for him, tending the grass out there in the field with such rigour he worked through supper, sometimes into the night. They did settle, though, never thinking there would be another war, not after that. John didn't. 'Can't just sit with the loss of it all,' he'd said. She had worried about how Albert would be after the second war. *Resilient is the word*, she thought. 'Bloody minded,' he'd say. Whenever he was on leave and then when he eventually came home it was as if he'd promised to remember every song and riddle he'd heard. Went looking for them, even. 'Got a new one from Jim at the market today.' Sometimes he took her to the cinema in Workington to learn the new song from a Western. Chanting it into work with young George, whistling around the cottage. *It was noisy to have that in the house*, she thought, *especially after years of him being away, but it helped George. Almost sang him into speaking again.* He'd been a quiet son before the second war, only seventeen when it broke out. After, he could weaken as pale as a swallow's egg.

But they'd come back. Wouldn't say luck, but they had come back. 'Miracle,' John might say. 'Miracle that plagues us to surrender to something. Pain of faith. Pain of doubt.' Albert would quote John sometimes after being in the first war together. Same regiment as most of the local men. Yes, it was good to think some of the stones had been clipped and wedged into that wall by Albert. When they were first there, they'd brought sheep and lambs into this back field if there was a problem with lambing. Hungry mouths suckling in twists and creaks, their mothers despondent by new demands. Such a small flock they had in those early days.

And they made more of them with the wool, milk and butter. Harold had to find his own way now. And he was doing well. Always finding a bid for the new way forward. Yes, Albert would be pleased they were still in it.

She felt the cover of her book. Thick leather curled the edges, waxed every now and then, never left to become brittle though the scored grain showed more over the years. And then, during the second war, the field became an allotment for turnips, carrots and cabbage. Albert helping Ada when he returned, never growing a lettuce that wasn't given over to slugs, fighting the rabbits, raking the leaves. Ada laughing at his jokes, working out his riddles. 'In the night, twists to the light,' he'd say. 'Lantern? Wolf? Primrose?'

Catherine shuffled in her chair and breathed, bible heavy in her hands. The air had a bite to it. She lifted the black ribbon and carefully spread the thin pages on her lap. A red squirrel scrummaged over the grass, tail poised, dowsing. It tunnelled into the leaves, crackling. The place had become a wilderness after Ada died, earth keeping the mosaic of her movements even when the vegetables had spread into weeds, ground slowly closing; George unable to watch. Ada had been part of their family long before she married George. She was eleven when she started to help with the butter and baking. George was six. After the war when he could hardly speak, Ada got him looking at maps. It was clever of her because tracing his time in Burma and John's in China seemed to help him come home. After a few months they were talking by the fire with an atlas, though he spoke rarely in between. But when Harold was born, it was as if George decided to be a father like Albert and joined in the banter. The three men inseparable and all as loud and familiar as a festival.

A gust lifted the thin pages of the bible. Yes, she'd sat there every year on Maundy Thursday, across from the old oaks, to wash the vanity of Absalom out of her. To remember the dark times with Christ, as if John were behind her, willing her on. 'Let it cleanse you, Catherine,' he would say. 'Remember the worst you've seen and lay it on your back to walk with Him. Then it's up to Christ to make a new world of it. Easter Sunday's the only strength able to lift the weight.' She thought of George. *He passed peacefully, that's the word for it*, she agreed, watching as if she were back in his old room. His head to the side, tight breaths after the stroke. Harold biting his lip in grief. They'd read John's letters to him. When she buried the letters with him, as he'd asked, it had been as if she passed him on to John.

And then the field had changed again. New soil. She looked up in surprise. Wasn't easy for Harold to dig up his mother's garden for Esther. There'd been grief in him, but he still did it. He was good. Last man standing. And Esther had put her back into the new garden. Digging, mulching and mixing in ashes, manure and roses. Banks of long grasses and reeds. Catherine had wondered what it was all for at the beginning. A year of earth dug over only to plant wild flowers. But then, the next Holy Week she'd sat there with her bible, she saw it had become a memorial garden. A memorial to the family, though Esther hadn't known it. *Would never tell her so*. Even the nettles blossomed, a taste she knew when she was young. Pleased to have it back.

She looked over to the fells. No clouds, just morning as far as she could trace. The leaves needed raking; she was surprised Esther hadn't cleared them, especially as the crocuses were pushing their green shoots around the snowdrops. Snowdrops, heads tilted with the love of a martyr. A raven landed on the oak tree; two feet together, unnatural, sweeping its wings for support, then silent black in silhouette.

Catherine looked at the page. She didn't like to dwell on things, just get on with the days. She felt pushed into this ritual every year. To remember the hard times. Always uncomfortable to think of the tragedy people went through. It was private. The oak trees looked silent. Isaiah said they gave *a crown of beauty instead of ashes . . . a garment of praise for heaviness.* He'd not wanted the mourners to be in despair. She straightened herself, *come on now Catherine*, and read, 'Then cometh Jesus with them unto a place called Gethsemane, and saith unto the disciples, Sit ye here, while I go and pray yonder.' She closed her eyes for a moment. *Betrayer.* She shook her head. *I never really sit with him. Prefer sleep. And it's to happen again.* She saw the image of crumbs on the bible. 'We're not worthy but only say the word,' she heard, bowing her head with a tut. *John would say even the crumbs from the altar are from Eden. But I'm not brave enough.* 'Take up your cross,' John would say, 'cleave to the Lord. Have your darkest memories beside Him and never alone.' And what wouldn't she remember for her Albert? She would go to the car with him and Ada and be gashed and worn with them if she could, waiting into the night to be found. She would be with him at his last breath, pray to know if he'd been awake for a while, kept warm, wet moustache, choking, watching the night, thinking of her. But she'd not be in the garden with Christ, she knew herself. Not tonight when He was to surrender His will, not to surrender her will too. Top of Calvary, waiting for them. Not sure Easter Sunday was beauty enough. Shouldn't have happened, never. Should be able to see Albert walking here with his great-grandson, such a young silky-haired boy, so quiet, as if he carried their silence. No, she wouldn't stay in that darkness. It shouldn't have been there in the first place. Nothing could change that. And she would have no new world without them.

'You old fool, Catherine,' she muttered. *Every year the same, every year. Never move on, even with a new family around you, always the same vigil. If they knew how caught up in it you were, they'd laugh.* She smiled. 'Never tell,' she said. 'They don't understand it nowadays.'

She looked over the garden again, black book weighing on her thighs and leant towards the roses; pleated buds soon in scent. Things were different now with young Stephen. She owed him too. Always in debt, she knew that. And Harold, putting his back into the farm like his father, often tired and never a moment. But young Stephen – well, she breathed as if the roses were in bloom. She would fill young Stephen with history. *Give him his family*, she thought. *No surrender, no giving it all away, no handing it over to Christ to do His will with it. That's my pledge this year. That's staying awake in the garden. Keep what's rightfully ours.* Christ would have to be happy with that.

*

Evening came and she was at the vigil with Esther and her mother. Wooden pew, cold stone darkness. It was harsh, always harsh when the altar was stripped of its woven front and long white linen cloths leaving bare grey slate. Two candles withering in draughts, a monstrance wrapped in white, same linen as last year, bound like cloth in the tomb, slowly carried down the aisle and laid between the candles. Even Mary couldn't look down on it, her eyes shrouded in purple.

Sunday before last had begun the same, with every statue covered. Stained glass of Mary and Martha above the altar curtained with two purple strips. The church had become dusk. Revd Patterson preached that it was the Lord calling them to look inward before winter fully passed and light came back into the mornings. But there were no morning prayers through the week like there used to be, just a silent walk to the church for readings one evening. And tonight they were there to stay, in the dark, without colour, without altar cloth, without moss or lichen on the bare stone, without rust from streams or new shoots, waiting. *No mistake*, she thought: *behind that bare altar, salvation comes from the East.* She'd seen it brighten the fell tops, sunrise striding firm in splendid slices against the shade, fixing a lit, boned edge to the sky; a weathered hand outstretched. Her brother John felt it in the mountains. Just before dawn, John would say, and he would be right. Before dawn came the shroud, the veil, rising for a moment, a quiet trace left on stone and then she remembered her promise: *keep young Stephen's family alive, fill the silence in him.*

They stayed there, all three in a row, blankets on knees, into the night, sometimes remembering and then resting, losing time or questioning. Lifting their eyes from the dark to the bare altar, staring into it as though somewhere behind, far into the valley was the hidden Christ, bound in His fate, calling for their strength, their loyalty, lifting their faces, gently, from the shame of broken hopes.

At about eleven-thirty Esther's father came to join them after his shift at the Manor. He woke Esther up as he sat on the end of the pew, fidgeting. His loud movements whisking the air after three and a half hours of silence, turning the pages of his bible like a Sunday paper. And they all left after midnight, a trail of cars in the dark, only a few walking as Catherine used to.

The next morning when it was still dark, Catherine dug out the suitcase from under her bed as she did every Good Friday and wiped it down with a damp cloth, her red fingers chilled. She clunked the metal clasps open and unfolded a blue jacket and a yellowed christening gown, moved aside the leather darts holder, large pocket knife and silver clothes brush and carefully pulled out a bundle of light blue cloth. When everything but the cloth was neatly back, she wrapped herself in a shawl, bedsocks and woollen hat, her breath white in the cold, and sat, blankets pulled up, to unwrap and then untie, oh so fingertip gently, the pile of letters. Some in cotton frayed envelopes, curled writing greyed at the edges, others bent in waves of yellowed rice paper, crackling to the touch, held together with ribbons now squinting deep red only within the ruffles of past knots. She picked one out from under the first few to start, so that it would be a surprise.

Longtan Medical Centre
Central China
21ˢᵗ January 1924

Dear Catherine,

The reason for my lapse in correspondence with you has been a snowstorm, which rested with us for a few days and has left us isolated for what will be a matter of months. The blizzard was filled with what I can only describe as the strength of creation. I confess I wondered if we had crossed the line up here in the peaks dwelling in a land too majestic for man. But our two donkeys and fowl were brought into the hallway while all people gathered into the Men's wing and stayed under the shadow of Our Lord's wings in prayer and bible reading, which brought comfort, even though our patients do not speak English. Many of us are still working hard to gain even the basic of conversations in local dialects without result. There were moments when the heavens were in such a rage we wondered if part of our roof had been lost. But after three days, the storm stopped as quickly as it came and peace rested on the land in the form of a vast and heavy white landscape in clear crisp sunlight.

You will be pleased to know we have managed to keep the generator going, so we still have heat. Some feared we would freeze, but with Mr Connolly's engineering and my brute force and checks throughout the night, all has been well. The difficulties between

certain people here have been eased by the situation.
Many of our brothers and sisters are giving thanks daily,
as it has cut us off from other villages or towns and so
we have remained clear of the terrible plague and the
groups of bandits I have previously mentioned. However,
I know that God loves truth, Catherine, and I know the
truth in addition to these blessings is that there are
people down in the valley who can't make it to the
hospital and will die because of it or will try the local
medicine and be rendered untreatable. Others will suffer
from the desperation of the bandits. No amount of
Gospel preaching will change that fact. So, while I marvel
at the scale of beauty here, I am troubled by the spiritual
fervour with which people's faith is renewed. I wonder
if relief is confused with faith, and I am concerned that
there will be a spiritual low when the snows melt. For
myself, though, God is good. I still hear Him in the
mountains and have taken time to dig trails for walks.
I can't pretend I don't wonder at His blessings and when
I think of the men who can't see this beauty, I am ever
broken. War must never be forgotten, though pain is a
heavy weight. But the Lord's work is to be found and
there is hope in helping these people. His path is not
for me to know or understand, I live with that, and
continue to practise, morning and night.

> *Holy Spirit, light divine,*
> *Shine upon this heart of mine;*
> *Chase the shades of night away,*
> *Turn the darkness into day.*

I will write often, knowing that you will receive a few letters together after the snow, but you will know that I continue to write, just as you and Albert remain in my prayers.

May God bless you and keep you.
John

V

Spring 1981

Harold

Harold strode up the side of Ard, the sound of his son behind, smaller steps. Now he was five, Stephen could walk behind and keep up, in line with the men, as Harold had done when he was a boy. He could almost see his own father's slow, deep-booted strides in front. Dark hair splayed under the back of his cap, chest out to the wind, singing. Until now, Harold needed to see Stephen in front, alert to the sight of him: small lad cutting into the fells, lifting his stride, tumbling and bouncing back, Harold reaching out, yanking him over 'eye up', if he got stuck through the ferns. Now his ears felt peeled, bare skin listening. No, he wouldn't look back, but he could hear the crackle and swish as if it were a scent. Was Stephen's head bowed, following his steps, looking at the back of his dad's boots, or was he looking out at the view? Best not to turn. He felt his father in front of him again. His chest ruffled out and he sank into his steps, following, watching the memory, walking. He would stop at the juniper tree and take a look.

He grabbed a fern leaf and then as the path turned he

tapped the old juniper, twisted as it leant out. *Takes a full strength to lie over the ground like that without support,* he thought, and then he turned. Stephen looked up. He'd stopped, waiting in line behind him. Blue eyes of his mother.

'All right, lad?'

'Aye,' he said with the nod of an old farmer.

'Well then,' Harold turned back and carried on, shouting 'Tap the old juniper and then let's have a singalong.' And they did, to the wind, low and solid up the hill.

At the top of the path before the peak Harold stepped to the side.

'Got your stone?'

'Aye.'

'Go on then, son. Up ye farrow. Take ye over Ard to look into Sail if ye like.'

'Oh aye,' Stephen replied, digging his feet into the climb as if it were natural to go over to the mines on Sail, nothing special. Harold let him go on a while and then, bending low, he ran, arms wide.

'Go on then!' he growled in a low roar.

Stephen squealing, not looking back, racing his little legs over tufts and sods to get to the peak before his father could catch him.

And at the top they clipped their stones into the cairn and sucked in the air, the view lifting their breath like the hook of a wave; sky widening them, stretching their fingers.

'Upside down, Dad.'

'Upside down?'

'Aye.' He held his arms up for his father to take and swing.

'A full 360?'

'Aye,' he giggled.

'Well then.' His father approached as if to tickle the bare belly showing from his stretch.

Stephen shuffled back, pulling his top down, laughing.

'No, Dad!' he giggled, as if being tickled. 'Upside down,' he spluttered as his father hovered, his laughter bumbling his small belly so deep it was infectious. And with a hurrumph, like biting an apple he had won at a fair, his father whisked him up by his ankles, striding out to the view, and jiggled him.

'What's that one, eh?'

'Red Pickle.' He laughed.

'Red Pickle is it, eh?' and Harold started to swing him, his son's laughter bubbling, defiant feet wriggling.

'H-e-e-l-vell-e-nnn!' Stephen tried to say whilst laughing and swinging.

'Oh Helvellyn is it?' he said slowly starting to spin.

'H-h-ho-o-ollvelle-nnnnn!'

'Oh, it's ho ho ho vellen is it?' and he grabbed his son's back and swooped him up, cradling him and shaking his head over him. 'Ho ho vellen.'

He put him down. 'Come on yer daft old thing,' he said with a tap on his bottom. 'Let's get over to Sail and see what tales Grandad has for us up there.'

Stephen pulled up his trousers, stumbling slightly before he found his step. 'We're off to Egypt now, Dad. I'll take ye this way.'

'Right you are, lad,' he said following. 'Oh, what about them camels ... ? We not going on them?'

'You're riding them, Dad.'

'Oh aye, of course!' He looked out over to Robinson as if sharing the irony with a spouse. 'Mine's a bad hoof.'

Stephen stopped and put his hand to his chin and looked down. 'Well then now, um . . .' And to his father's amazement he walked back up to him and bent down, circling his hand. 'There. That'll do it,' he said seriously.

'Great. Oh yes, much better now. Thank you. On we go.'

'Aye. On we go!' Stephen called as he marched forward, knees up, arm high in the air as if flying a flag.

A few weeks later, hands numb after another walk, they shivered by the fire, towelling, soaked from a spring storm. Wind rattled the chimney, searching into the hollow, sieving the heavy pellets of water before clattering them onto the roof, like seeds on stone. Stephen stretched his soft arms out to be rubbed. Even his forearms and shoulders were red. Harold rubbed into the numb, knowing his small chunky hands and feet would go through an ache and then sting before they rested warm again.

'Come on, blow out, make a roar, lad,' he said blowing through his lips like a motor. 'The storm'll be in ye, lad. Got to shake it out.'

And when they were flushed almost with fever heat, sitting wrapped in sheepskin by the fire, they rested in silence, a smoky peace between them, hot Ribena and tea, letting the crackle and light from the flames remind them of the walls, the stone, home.

That week Harold had a bad chest, but Stephen breezed through without a sign of it. *Must be getting old*, Harold thought, the spring and autumn colds getting to him more as the years passed. Still, with dipping not long done between the rains and lambing only just starting, he could work it off in the fells. *Good check on ewes'll sort out this damned head and shake the weakness out of these legs.* Joe drove into the yard and Harold nearly passed with a tip of his hat, keen to walk on but stopped to ask 'All well, Joe?'

'No it's bloody not.'

'Oh, what's that?'

'Bloody field's drenched.'

'New one by Robinson?'

'Aye, t'beck's backed in through troughs.'

'Flooded?'

'Mostly near the beck, but a good part is drenched. Their bloody "only approve twenty-two yard spacing" when it should have been eleven.'

'How's that, then? Beck blocked or summat?'

'Aye it's high but it'll have been high over the winter and not flooded like this. Weathered the bank away. What field between a mountain and a beck needs the least pipes? Just have to look at the contours of a map to see it, but oh no. I said it at the time, before they dug the pipes in for drainage, I said that we needed the tightest spacing and the most pipes because of the fell, but, young bloody Ministry official decided it had "natural incline" and not eleven feet between pipes but twenty-two. The widest gap! Got our field confused with a bloody cricket pitch.'

Harold's chest tightened. Holding his breath. Without hay they were lost. They couldn't afford to buy it in, not this year. They stood in silence, Joe coughing into a spit.

'I'll have to get them to come back,' Harold said in a low voice, thinking out loud.

'No,' Joe said, coughing again, 'we've not time. We'll be put on a rota and they'll get to us in a few months. We'll have to dig it through ourselves and build a bank to stop water coming over. Flood's a flood. Waits for no man.'

'Right,' Harold said slowly. 'Been bad with rain, but.'

'Rotting, lad, unless we drain it ourselves. Just need to think.'

'Right, best see it, then,' Harold said, stepping onto the side of the tractor; engine rolled to start down the yard. Every bounce pressed on his eyes, the weight of air pushing against his head as he leant out, his grip of the door, searching with blurred view over the fields to the beck as if he might find a cause.

They left the tractor at the gate, and part way through the fields the lines, which used to drain the soil towards the beck, now lay like clay troughs filled with water. Further along, Joe was right, the tide had filled the ground with mounds of silt and mud, cradling the water in, and further up again, the bank had weathered away so that the beck poured in like a tributary.

'The water'll never get out again,' Harold said, his heart starting to thump in his chest, his hands shaking. 'You seen any of this last year?'

'Oh, I thought it'd come till that. I'm telling ye, nothing like this last year,' Joe said, nearly shouting.

'What about winter? It can't have just come in a flash.'

'Flood likely. Summat changed on the fell.'

Harold felt confused. 'What flood?'

Joe looked at him as if he was making a point, but all Harold felt was frustration. 'No, Joe. I mean when with the rains.'

'When it flooded?'

'Aye,' he said pressing in to keep his focus, an angry wave of heat racing to his head. 'The angles can't just go wrong like that.'

'Angles? That's the problem lad, there aren't any. They've sliced bloody straight lines into land that curves off a fell.' Joe said, meeting Harold's eye. Harold stared back at Joe to keep his focus.

'No bother,' Joe said, a stern look on his face. 'I'll sort it. You get back to the fells.' He turned and waded off, hands in pockets.

Harold's face fired up, his skin burnt. Joe was too far off now to talk to and he hadn't the energy to shout. *Leave him for a while*, he thought, feeling words in the heat of his head like soup. *He must feel embarrassed about it. It's his field to sort. Leave him.* But, no, he should go after him and get it sorted.

'We don't have time for this. Come on, you bugger,' he said to himself. 'Just walk alongside him for a while and chew it through.' But when he pushed into a stride his chest hung as if it were nothing but his shirt in the wind, and he needed to lie down, just for a moment, his ankles weakening, a swish-crunch of grass sounding around him, fever warming him into rest, the sky so bright it lingered in his eyes, leaving him in wait.

Must get to Joe, he thought, and pressed against his own ribs, a shout of frustration building and then lost at once by his grained breath sifting, turning him gentle, a small wheeze to gasp through, needing to be delicate for a moment, heart racing. *Oh no*, he thought, sky in his eyes, any movement tightening his chest. An echo of the tractor engine moving away, small drops of rain tapering on his face, a welcome coolness to his shirt.

It was two weeks now that Harold had been in bed. Felt longer. Stephen checking on him in the mornings.

'Good night's rest, Dad?'

'Very good night, that one, and yoursel'?'

'Very good night, that one,' he replied, sidling himself into the bed, his bare feet wriggling.

'What you got on today, lad?'

'Bring A Story Day.'

'Bring A Story Day? Well, have you got one?'

He shook his head and looked up to Harold, eyes open as a moon, waiting, happy to be waiting for something.

'Got an idea?'

Stephen hummed for a moment. 'Noddy in the Sweet Shop.'

'Noddy in the Sweet Shop? Now there's a good story,' he said and at the sound of Esther's feet coming upstairs with breakfast, Harold threw the covers open for him to hide.

'Here you are, love,' she said, tray just about to be balanced on his knees, but put safely on the chest of drawers. She smiled at Harold. 'You ready for school, Stephen?' she called down the corridor, trying not to laugh with the sound of Stephen's giggles under the blanket. Harold ruffled his hand underneath and gave him a tickle.

'Where's Stephen?' Esther asked and Harold tickled again.

'I'm in my bedroom!' he answered.

'Oh, he's in his bedroom.'

'Yes,' came from under the blankets.

'Oh, are you now?' Esther teased, which brought the reply, 'Yes, yes!'

'You getting your story ready for today?' Silence from the blankets. 'Where are you?' she called.

'Noddy in the Sweet Shop!' he called and Harold tickled him again, making him sit up like a mound in the bed.

'Noddy in the Sweet Shop, indeed!' she said as the blankets slid off his ruffled hair, making them all laugh, and Esther turned to collect the tray.

'No, I'll take it,' Stephen called, scrambling off the bed, and Harold watched as he wobbled the tray over to him, boiled egg steady in its cup. 'Now that's a good breakfast,' he said, sounding like Harold.

'Thank you,' Harold said, somehow disarmed by his son serving him, not knowing quite what to do next.

'Want a bit?'

Stephen looked up to Esther. 'Can I, Mam?'

She shook her head. 'You've had yours, love.'

'Can I have mine in here?'

She looked over at Harold and he felt blank.

'Don't see why not for a couple of days,' she said.

Stephen smiled. 'We can both have boiled eggs.' And Harold felt emptied, wanting them to leave the room, so they wouldn't see the tremor in his hand, the sharpness in his sight, the frustration at the stark outlines of their faces, which had not yet left from the fever. He couldn't hold it back for much longer. His son patted him on the arm and Harold felt guilt as he longed to be back at an early breakfast, mulling the day's work with Joe, or silent. No thoughts, none of these fevered thoughts, just planning their way into the land.

'Better get your story now and do your chores – eggs checked. We'll sort breakfast for tomorrow,' Esther said to Stephen who sulked a little as he left the room. Esther sat on the side of the bed, as she had done every morning, not watching while he ate, telling him about the news of her mother who was getting worse and had been found wandering around the estate. 'She refused to come home. Thought Dad was trying to trick her, he said. Didn't know him. Just can't think of her going into care, but she'll have to.' She leant towards the corridor: 'Ten minutes, darling, and then we're off!'

'Just there!' Stephen shouted.

She touched Harold's forehead and took his hand, which made him flinch. The skin had swollen again and was bleeding a little in parts. He knew he looked back at her without a thing to say, but had no strength for more.

'Stephen?' she called into the air, piercing Harold's ears.

'Think I'll sleep now, love,' Harold said.

'Do you need a hand, Stephen?'

'Just there, Mam!' he called back again.

Harold leant his head back.

'Your head OK?' she asked.

'Aye, fine, just resting.'

'Not hungry?'

'Be downstairs tomorrow, love,' he said, watching Esther for clues, not knowing how possible it was. The doctor wasn't telling him everything. Never ill from a day in the rain before, and the doctor saying it might be the new virus going around didn't help. They didn't even know what a virus was. No explanation even for the sore rash on his arms and chest. No cure, only rest. He just wanted to push through or sleep till it was over and then get back to work.

'Joe has asked for breakfast a little later for a while, so he can get more work done; if you feel like it, we could have you down for about nine-thirty when I come back from taking Stephen to school.'

Her voice seemed further away now and what she said seemed rehearsed. Joe would never ask for food later than he had a chance to eat, not if he'd been up since five, but it would be a plan they'd all come to. It embarrassed him that they'd done that. No need for fuss. But he couldn't be doing with them hovering in his room. Made his fever worse.

'That'll do for a start,' he said.

'Just a bit at a time, though, OK?'

'No bother,' he said falling into a sleep, dizzy in the fells.

Later that morning, Catherine came in, bustling round the bed with a pile of ironed clothes for the chest of drawers. She stood at the window for a while. Harold was glad she didn't talk, felt pleased to have her there, almost brought the view into the room.

After a while she said, 'Albert had a fever and he didn't make sense for a month. Too much heat in him, but it settled. Short walk this afternoon'd do you good. Clear the mind.'

'I'll not want to upset Esther.'

'No, I'll talk to her, lad. She's just worried about you with all these new viruses going round. I'll be up for you about three, all right?'

'Very good,' he said, wondering if he would have enough strength. 'Fells'll bring it out of me,' he mumbled, looking up quickly to see if he was alone in the room.

He woke slightly at some point and saw Catherine sitting by him reading what looked like a letter and then slept again, waking when it was dark. He felt himself agree to something through a drunken head, 'can put the hogs back onto the fell once we've the ewes in with the rams,' he said and next woke in the coldness of the night, Esther sleeping beside him, feeling darkness in his sight. The silence in the room was empty.

He must have slept at some point. Once it had been light for a while, Stephen came in.

'Good night, Dad?'

'Good one, that, and you?'

'Good one, that,' he said, climbing into the bed, Esther following him in with two eggs on two trays.

'You warm enough, love?' she asked.

'Aye,' he said, looking up to her, realising his face was damp.

'You look a little cold,' she said and touched his brow. 'Cold,' she said again and Stephen leant around in front of him, looking at his eyes, and put his hand on his cheek. 'Cold, Dad. You need another blanket?'

'No thanks, son,' he said, looking down at the tray. 'Just need a good egg.'

'Crack it for you?' Stephen asked in Esther's voice and Harold looked up to Esther, who saw his discomfort.

'Come on now, eat your breakfast while it's hot,' she said and Stephen settled next to him, legs outstretched, ready for his tray.

A few months later, Harold was back at work, the September morning lit white along the edge of the fells, frost drawing the brightness down into the fields, cattle snorting mist and sheep bustled by crisp hedges. He was still weak in his chest, felt it in the steep climbs, but pushed into a steady plod. Best medicine: never felt more himself than when he was out here. It was as if the grass reached towards him. He walked over to the old juniper and leant on its craned trunk. Sap bulged from under its bark, turning to rust. *Buckled under the pressure. Not easy without windbreak up here. But they give a good shelter, I'll give them that.* A good omen, his grandfather would say, to have one so near home.

When Harold got back, Stephen was in the yard waiting, his light brown hair thin in the wind, narrow blue eyes fixed ahead.

'Come on, lad, do your jacket up now!' he shouted, climbing, sore-hipped, into a pen at the bottom of the yard. He ducked out of view to check the stray sheep and watched through the cracks as the boy obediently fumbled with his zip, pulling the hood over so his face was flanked, and then ran his small feet across the uneven cobbles like shaking seeds. Then, fence grabbed, feet kicked in, he climbed to stretched arms, swaying slightly in balance at the top of the bars as if the wind rocked him.

'A minute, lad,' his father said, staying low on the other

side so that the sheep would accept the food. He swept some hay towards her, building a circle, and then gently stroked her. 'There now, lass.' Pulling up her fleece to see if her ribbed belly was clear of sores.

'Why's her fleece so long, Dad?'

'Must have been lost at the front of a storm. But Hemp found her. He's a magician is your new Hemp.'

'When?'

'Evening count yesterday. Got her to me, back legs not working well, but she's here, lass, aren't you? Here now. We'll have to thank Ronnie,' he said, nodding at Stephen. 'He's found you a good'n.'

'Ronnie said he put a penny on Hemp's nose when he came out for luck.'

'Must be it, then,' he said, looking over in a quiet laugh, keeping low as he went towards his son, whose arms were quivering now to keep himself up.

'Getting big now,' he said, lifting him over, noticing a thin purple line around his mouth from blackberries. 'Be a man soon.'

The ewe craned her shaggy neck from fear of the movement, matted wool trailing in the hay, her legs now limp. They bent together, the sound of wind softening behind the fence, and waited.

'Aye, she's doing well,' Harold whispered, feeling Stephen put his small arm around his neck. The sheep tried to push away, wriggling, her boned legs still not moving. 'Hey now lass, all right, all right now,' he cooed in a warm louder voice. 'Bit wild this'n.'

'Why's she wild, Dad?' he whispered hot into his ear.

'On the fells without company for ower long.'

'How long?'

'Oh well now, a year or more somewhere far away.'

'How far?'

'About as far as other side of Crummock, towards Mellbreak or so, might have had a fall, found a cave I would say. She's a fighter.' And Stephen crept forward, carefully patting her fleece, the ewe accepting him, not moving. 'All right there now, lass,' he said quietly and moved a little hay into the circle. 'Why she stay over there?'

'Never know the ways,' Harold said, both of them watching her breath.

'She well, Dad?'

'She'll be to recover unless it's her time. We'll hope on her, anyhow.'

'Not going to take her away?'

'No, they'll not want this'n.'

A week later, Harold was in for breakfast and Joe was looking tired. Snow had cut heavy into autumn. Rare it was so early, but you could never predict it. This time at the end of gathering them off the fell with the other farmers, they'd had more than usual go astray. Looking for shelter or confused. They'd built the herd up to nearly 370 now and it was a push to hem them in for the autumn dip. He'd have to do it on the right date and take the right time, even with this snow, or he wouldn't get checked off.

When the dip came, it was heavy work, hot even with another line of snow newly settled. But jacket off and sleeves rolled up, he lifted some, pushed others, baptising them all to keep them safe, Stephen running about helping Joe hold the ramp, keeping them nuzzled at his back till his dad was ready. Occasionally helping him dip. Esther was at the other end of the line, herding them into the fenced run from the yard, metal bars pushing into the fuzz of wool, lambs poking their heads out and banging into the bars as the weight of the sheep moved them on, hammering their bleats. And along the line the three dogs simmering before a pounce, a light snow on their backs.

A car drew up and a Ministry man got out and leant on the gate for a while, watching.

'Policeman, Dad,' Stephen shouted over the noise. Harold didn't know what to do, so called a halt, Joe and Stephen pushing back the bolting sheep.

'Esther,' he called, nodding towards the gate, still fenced in and straddled over the dip. She brought him up.

'Hello there?' he said, as the Ministry man came nearer, knowing he'd said it as a question.

'Jack Sutherland,' he said.

'He's from Waverton,' Esther said.

'Well, been there a year or two but working Cockermouth area now.'

'Oh aye,' Harold said still with a question on his face. 'All OK?'

'Yes, I'll just find myself a place, don't mind me.'

'Right.'

'We'll look over the paperwork later, if that's OK.'

'Yes, be no trouble,' Harold chimed, looking over at Joe then back, watched by the clean shirt and jacket, straightening himself, giving Stephen a look and soon feeling the next ewe shoot to the back of his legs.

After hours of work, Harold's arms and chest stung, wet shirt, splashing them in, spray of cold water sometimes burning his mouth. Metal stick in hand, he pushed their noses under, often resorting to his welly boot. Most struggled, panicked, needing him to delve in and wrench their soaked wool out, wiry in his hand. Stephen liked getting wet, but he didn't like to be kicked, so Harold kept him back. By the end of the day, the yard and two nearest fields were filled with sheep standing soggy legged, spotted in snow, patches of icy sludge webbing their backs. And now, paperwork handed over, Harold was by the hearth for a late supper, right eye swollen but sitting legs out front, next to his tired son, hot-cheeked and chafed, stinging hands, biting into chunks of yeasty bread dunked into a bowl of Catherine's stew. Soon digging into hot, sweet, crab apple and blackberry crumble with milky cream.

VI

Spring 1984

Esther

Her hands were cold kneading the dough. She was used to them being warm, too hot sometimes, but they felt cold against the warm dough, making it flat. She wiped them on her apron and headed upstairs, ankles itching. *Must lose weight*, she thought, as she turned into Stephen's room to check his school clothes were ready. He was in the bathroom. She opened his curtains; the poster of Bobby Charlton scoring a goal shone in red gloss. Champion the Wonder Horse, Batman, Marineman and the Six Million Dollar Man covered the rest of the walls. *Most colourful place in the house*. His old bear was in his bed, radio by the side. She hadn't seen the bear there for a year or so, and pulled the blankets over, leaving it buried in case he didn't want her to know. Someone walked past and into Catherine's room. 'Everything all right?' she called. When she peered in Harold was crouching by the bed surprised at the sight of her. 'Everything all right?'

'Well, aye,' he said, straightening. 'Just checking for Trin.'

'Can I help?'

'All sorted,' he said and walked past.

Following him down the stairs her knees felt empty and she was glad of the banister.

'Paperwork to be sorted for the dipping again today,' Esther said to Catherine as she put the plates out for the sausages and eggs, the smell of charred fat filling the kitchen, making the air stick. 'Started a few days ago and keeps getting put to the side. Seems a lot, twice a year.'

Catherine tutted, watching the meat fall awkwardly as she piled it on, and they walked through, plates in hand, Stephen standing from his seat to tuck in his shirt.

'Collar out,' Esther said, watching his neck immediately stretch and fingers fumble to straighten it.

'"Sullen", Harry Marsh called the new double dipping regulations. He knows he's got the same Ministry man coming with a stopwatch again,' Harold said with an outbreath. 'I can't think straight being watched like that. Once in autumn is bad enough. Now we've more than the hogs to dip in spring, they'll be watching for at least a day.'

'"Sullen" is it, and what's that when it's at home?' Joe laughed.

'Bloody paperwork,' he said, looking to Catherine, pursing his lips with the familiar recompense for swearing.

'"Sullen", have till remember that,' Joe said with a cheeky lilt.

'Now then, enough of that.'

'Aye, well,' Joe muttered, tucking in. 'Get the better of whoever we have when he arrives. Might be lucky and have a local bobby to come and help instead. Do you know which?'

'No. Won't think on it till it happens,' Harold said, leaning towards Stephen with a nod. 'Keep the hope, that's it.'

'Aye, better get forms done,' Joe added, 'or we'll all be ... well, sullen!'

Harold looked over at Joe, whose shoulders were bouncing slightly in a quiet laugh.

'Beat you at balling this year,' Harold said to Joe, nodding at Stephen.

'Early crop, Dad, be with us soon,' Stephen said.

'That's right, lad, best year. Beat him no problem, with a little help from my lad, here.'

'Two against one won't even do it! You can try with your tricks, but you'll not catch my coat tails.'

'We'll see,' Harold said, winking at Stephen. He was pale from the spring cold he got every year – so many farmers were getting it now.

'They've banned the chlorines now so we'll be using the new one for the inspector. Were right about it in the food chain, likely.'

'Where did you hear that?'

'I have my ways!'

'That club, likely.'

'If by "that club" you mean the Pint Club in the local, then maybe.'

'No, I mean that socialist thing you go till.'

'Oh, well now, good job someone's there listening to what's going on!'

Harold shook his head. 'Well, we've been using the right one for a while anyway.'

Esther looked at Joe and he smiled. She saw his banter

and movements protected Harold. Sometimes she felt outside their world. Simpler without her.

'But they're not coming this Saturday?' Catherine asked.

'No, no, we've registered for dipping two weeks Saturday. Even they wouldn't dare come to our Catherine's farm on Lazarus Saturday, they know better.'

Catherine smiled.

'You be tying a slice of cloth then, on Saturday?' Joe asked Stephen.

Stephen looked at Esther.

'I think he has some friends coming round.'

'Aye, well it's different for the kiddies now, eh?' Joe said.

'You do it?' Stephen asked.

'Well, I did when I was a lad.' Joe looked to Catherine. 'And I'm glad Catherine does it for us. But you're with us in a couple of weeks?'

'Oh aye,' Stephen called.

'Might get you showing that townie inspector how a young'un can dip, if you like.'

'Yes, right,' he said, his fists lifted for the challenge.

'We'll keep you right lad, no bother,' Harold said.

'You in, Missus?'

'No, not this time,' Esther said without a plan, quickly adding, 'Be with Mother, but I thought you might ask Clive to come up for the day.'

'Oh, bit short notice.'

'Well, we'll see,' she said, purposely not looking in Catherine's direction. 'I'll call him today and let you know.'

'Good old Clive. Not used to sheep is Clive, with all them milkers,' Joe said, leaning over to Stephen. 'We'll have him filtering them through the pens in your mam's place, and leave the man's job at the dip to you, my lad!'

Esther glanced at Stephen, straightening in her chair, watching him copy her without looking. And for a moment the table seemed vivid, the room shaping around them. *Might not be perfect but it's the best of things*, she thought, wanting to hold onto the picture, feeling her rough fingernails, wondering why she spent time worrying when it seemed to make no difference. *Just have to live it.* She wondered what Harold had been looking for in Catherine's room. Strange that it bothered her.

Once they were all out and Stephen on his bus, Esther sorted the pile of sewing she had to do for the Millers by the end of the week and went upstairs. She was doing alteration work now, just for locals who asked, and more work was coming in, which was good. Before she cleared Stephen's room, she went into the old room that had been hers before they were married. *Stephen will probably move here. Maybe when he changes school. It's a little bigger, and if he wants it then, well, it looks as if there are no others joining him, so he may as well.* She'd been told by the doctors to keep trying, but no pregnancy settled longer than two or three months. She sat, heavy in her hips, on the edge of the bed and looked out towards the garden. It could still happen. Stephen was eight already. Hard to believe it had passed so quickly, but there he was. Such a different child to her. She was more like her grandmother, and for a moment she remembered her grandmother walking, quiet steps in the leaves. Taking Esther into the Manor gardens, 'Nothing wrong with a bit of rain', letting her run around the rhododendrons to hide and loop back to find her again at a steady pace. Never picking flowers unless they were in the fields or woods. She looked around the room. Her grandmother's had been small, but they still fitted a chair next to the chest of drawers, though it only opened so far. Enough room for Esther to sit, holding wool or knitting. Yes, her grandmother had a steady pace, she thought watching the clouds, and Esther had been like her and quiet, so quiet, she used to say people went silent around her. When she helped with her dried flower arrangements, it was as if they were dreaming together. Her mother would pass now and then. 'Don't see why we need another,' or 'Be good to have some real work around here.' But her grandmother kept folding the flowers in, her pile of darning always done on time. And she kept secrets as if they were delicate. Like the first wash after Easter Sunday. When her mother left the room, her grandmother would open the washing machine lids and quickly mix in a fist full of salt, leaning over them with a prayer to keep their work protected till next spring. Her strong hands pulling the clothes horse up with the first linen, hooking the rope in, sheets hanging over the machines. 'Salt will stop you being Lot's wife,' she'd whisper. Esther thought of Catherine in the kitchen. She was more stoic about her small rituals, here and there, and Esther never liked to ask.

Sitting room straightened and kitchen cleared, Esther headed up to the allotment to check on the squirrel holes, slugs and weeds. She liked the routine of marching up there. It was time to seed for a good crop. She took a large pot of tea with her, covered in not one but two knitted warmers, and a metal bucket. After digging out a new section, she stretched her back and warmed her red fingers around a cup steaming in the morning chill, fingernails muddied, palms sore. She looked over to the garden. She hadn't tended to it for so long it showed. Hardly noticed walking through it. The carefully placed chair in line with the oak trees must have been Catherine. She put the cup down and bent back to work; should put her gloves on really, she thought, but she'd only be peeling hard skin from hard skin, and she liked the feel of the soil. *Life's brought out the tomboy in me.*

On the drive to the rest home in Cockermouth, she wondered what she should do about her mother at the weekends. Her father found it hard to look after her now. He had to trust that if she went out at night and he didn't wake up, she would wander home again and not leave the Manor grounds. Most of the gates were locked. *She could stay here, at the farm,* Esther thought, *in the spare room. Could make a bed on the floor for me next to her, just for one night a week. It wouldn't be too bad. Father could come up for Sunday morning to see her and Saturday evening if he wanted.* But there would be no laundry room, no old kitchen, no familiar chair for her mother by the fire, no Manor gardens. She took a breath. *She'll be anxious without her things. Holds onto them like a map. Home is more company for her than any of us.*

When Esther got to St Anne's, her mother was in her room, not wanting the noise of the television.

'Sounds terrible,' she said. 'Sirens and shouting. Terrible in there.'

'But it's nice to sit with the others sometimes, Mam,' she said, and her mother looked up disapprovingly.

'Well, how are you today?' Esther said.

'Not bad, we ready to go, then?'

'Go where?' she asked, knowing that she meant home.

'What we waiting for? Poor things in here, terrible. Who are we visiting now?' her mother asked, waiting a moment for a reply. Esther wondered what to say and, not finding an answer, her mother went on, 'Never want it, just terrible, now let's get on.'

'Would you like a cup of tea, Mam?' Esther asked as she took off her coat and settled in the chair. 'Be coming to the farm on Saturday for the night,' she said.

'The farm? Which farm?'

'My farm, our farm. You know, Harold, Stephen, our farm.' Her mother looked blank. 'Be nice to see Stephen, wouldn't it? He loves seeing you,' and still she saw no recognition of the name. She sighed. 'Saw Morris down street,' she said.

'Oh,' her mother lit up. 'How is he?'

'Not bad, getting some seeds from Dickinson's. He was with Geoffrey Pattinson.'

'Geoffrey, Margaret's boy?'

'Yes.'

Her mother rolled her eyes. *She's probably remembering him getting up to no good at the hound races*, Esther thought. *Not a penny and still a bet on!*

'Would you like a cup of tea?'

'Oh well, why not before we go.'

'They'll be in to offer tea in a minute,' Esther said to her mother, as she helped her back onto the bed.

Her mother shook her head. 'It's slow.'

'What do you mean, slow?'

'The service here, they're not very good.'

'They'll be busy, lots of visitors.'

'Well,' her mother said, still disapproving. 'Where exactly is this place?'

'Dad sends his love,' Esther said. Her mother looked blank. 'Do you know who I am?'

'Yes, of course.'

'What's my name?'

'Well,' she said, patting the bedspread, 'Oh now, I've just forgotten. Is it Karen?'

'No, it's Esther, Mam. It's me, Esther.'

'Is it?' she said in surprise.

'Yes and Stephen's my son. You remember Stephen, Mam?'

'A son, do you?'

'Yes, of course, and he did a picture for you.' She rustled into her bag, looking up to see her mother's suspicious glance. And, picture of a fisherman in hand, she sat for a while, watching her mother get up and put her coat on ready to go.

'We're not leaving today, Mam,' she said. 'You need a little more rest first.'

'What is this place?'

'It's a rest home, Mam, just for a while. You need to be taken care of for a little while, you've not been well.'

'Haven't I? What was wrong?'

'Just a little thing the doctor needed to check, Mam, and nearly better now.'

'I'm fine,' she said. 'Let's go now and not be bothering with all that.'

The next morning Esther was in the allotment again, tying the netting, wondering how they could ask the Manor to secure the gates when her mother stayed without flagging up the danger. *Might be too worried to have her there. But it's the only gift worth anything to her.* She dug stones in to hold down the net and pushed them steady with her heel.

Maybe she could stay at the Manor with her mother, just once a week. But then she worried that Harold needed her. The other people she knew who had these viruses took a while to get over them and they came back. Worry spilled over her sometimes and she was getting used to it like cold in winter. That and the pain of not being able to be with her mother every day and help her father every day and Harold and Stephen and . . . she looked around, frustrated. *Spring doesn't seem enough sometimes,* she thought. *Bud and leaf, seducing you with new fruit. Hovering over the ground with hope as if it was always meant to be abundant. Tricking you into forgetting how ruthless life is, discarding the weak. What kind of beauty is that?*

She stood, easing her back, looking through the lattice partition to what she could see of her garden. The long grass and irises pierced through in speared bud. Elder and dock were beginning to lace and knot above the nettles; privet and vetch overgrown and dropping their buds; rose leaves looking speckled. *Like another place when you look through these squares. Hidden.* The old bench Joe and Harold had made for her needed varnishing again. The wind seemed to burn it off every other year. Well, the garden would wait till she had more time. Stephen had two friends over this Saturday. They'd probably play kick the can in the hayloft again. She had too much sewing to do, but she'd be sure to get a sponge cake in the oven for them.

That night she dreamt of her grandmother, standing in their old hallway with her wrinkled stockings and wide hips. She had a bunch of flowers; dried, light-pink roses, held them like a posy. And then she put a white handkerchief over them. Esther woke up, puzzled. They were the flowers her grandmother had kept in a box under her bed for special days. 'Be what's on the Pearly Gates,' she'd said when her father brought them home from the Manor display.

She lay awake, Harold snoring beside her, and remembered climbing up the ladder in the pantry when she was young to check those roses drying from the hooks in the ceiling. They dangled tight together, buds and blooms overhead. It was tricky to hold her position on the ladder at first but she'd become bird-like over the years. Pinching the back of the flower heads to see if they bounced like a soft drum, or felt dull like old paper. Looking into the tips for mildew or browning. Always careful that she didn't bruise the face of the petals, especially those roses.

'They'll not be much different from yesterday,' her mother would call if she heard the ladder grating against the stone floor again.

'Still pink as perfume, Grandma,' Esther would say, trotting into the bedroom after her check. 'Still pink as perfume.'

Esther's tears quietly wet her temples and into her hair.

She missed her. She felt ashamed that the farm was lonely. She was close to Harold, they depended on each other, cared for each other. But somehow the respect they had seemed to separate them. She'd thought intimacy would come with marriage. Wordless first. But they didn't have time to do more together than eat with the family. Never the energy for long evenings with maps and books. He was good with Stephen, playing cards. Listening to his homework without understanding the new maths. Interested even when she knew he was ill. Early bed. So tired his memory would go. It was admitting defeat to say that she was weary from looking after him. Especially when she knew he couldn't help it. That there was no one to blame had a weight of its own. She didn't have enough goodness in her sometimes and it made her feel lost. She'd started to think she was not frustrated with it all, just selfish. Hadn't realised she'd had ideas about how things would be until a few years had passed on the farm. Hopes for a private world with Harold where they might walk in the evenings or on a Sunday afternoon. Decorate the cottage with new colours, tapestries and dried flowers. Have their own projects after supper by the fire. Her mother had needed their house to stay the same, but Esther wanted, well, she wanted it to be different. *You're not a child any more Esther*, she chided herself. *Be grateful. You've more than you can count here.*

She tried to imagine talking to her grandmother about it and felt the relief of heading out for one of their regular walks. When her grandmother was older, about Catherine's age now, her arthritis was bad but she still enjoyed the woods, swinging her hips side to side to lift her step, toes bucked into her old shoes, the ones she said were the most comfortable. She couldn't bend easily, so Esther picked more flowers and grasses than before – just in case – storing them in her bedroom. 'Your room's more of a meadow than the hills,' her grandmother would say. Dust and crumbling petals settling around the edge of the floor, 'like salt for a newlywed'. They brought their own season, a distant summer, ever-coloured and evergreen. She thought of the dream. Why the white handkerchief? Why cover the roses? Harold turned, he was a light sleeper now with burning or swollen joints. A bit like her grandmother must have been. Uncomfortable on his side, snoring to wake himself on his back. She had to make sure she didn't touch him in the night. *Must sleep, there's a pile of sewing waiting.*

The next morning she was up before Harold and made Stephen's favourite ginger biscuits for school to share with his friends. Alterations on the latest clothes were started before breakfast was laid, quickly returned to after Stephen was on the bus.

'Have you seen my penknife anywhere?' Harold asked.

'No, where did you use it last?'

'I've looked there, but have you seen it around the house?'

'No, I haven't.'

'Well then.'

'I'll have a look if you like.'

'Aye, thanks,' he said, heading out to the yard. She got up to search, but soon thought of the people coming to have a second fitting the next day and the others coming to pick things up. She'd keep an eye out for it. Catherine passed with a bucket of soapy water to scrub the front porch. Every week in Lent and then every day in Holy Week 'to welcome a stranger'. Esther had promised to help with church cleaning in the afternoon, but she didn't have time. No, Catherine was getting frail, though she would never admit it. She had better go, and clean quickly, so she could sew again before supper. Otherwise, Catherine would be the only one there and she wouldn't stop till it was done.

The church was cold and the old lump of wax Catherine had brought took some rubbing in. Mixed with the oak it smelled roasted. It would have taken more elbow grease if Catherine hadn't been polishing from the beginning of Lent; as she had for about fifty years. She'd been known to get a ladder in to polish the wooden angels at the base of every ceiling beam. The pews almost belonged to her. In fact, her mother had brought her there, just after she was born. *Seventy-eight years of cleaning. Same pews, by the same windows.*

When the two women had finished, the light through the windows seemed to redden the wood. The small, carved organ at the foot of the aisle shone a burnished circle around its bronze flutes. As Catherine creaked on a pew to kneel at the front, Esther wondered if the wax made a difference to the sound. It seemed to. There was no doubt the church was peaceful when it was empty. A shaft of sun moved across the altar, it seemed to lift the dust. She'd never paid attention to the small section of red wings on the stained-glass windows above Mary and Martha. Eight of them folded around a face. *Must be Christ*, she thought, but then saw that the faces of Mary, Martha and Christ were the same. Martha's head was covered with a white shawl which reminded her of the white handkerchief in her dream. It gave her the feeling that she should make sense of it, but couldn't. She stacked the basket and other cleaning things at the foot of the aisle, hoping the sound of packing would move them towards home. But after a while, Catherine was still kneeling and an impatient need to get back to the farm took Esther up the aisle to sit next to her as a reminder. Catherine sat back and turned, a steel to her eye. 'Taken your confession this year?'

'No,' Esther replied, surprised by the question. 'Never have.'

'Never?'

'No. We didn't do it at our church.'

'Even when you were younger?'

'No, not even then.'

'Well, I don't suppose it matters.'

Esther sat for a moment, confused.

'If I get you the words, would you help an old woman?' Catherine said wryly.

'I wouldn't know how.'

'Well, dear, just say the words and the Lord will do the rest. This priest hasn't time to do it more than once a month in Lent for an old-fashioned one like me, but it would save me doing it on my own,' she said with a neat smile. 'If you would.'

'Will it take long? Only we do need to get back soon,' Esther said, feeling embarrassed at her frustration.

'About ten minutes,' Catherine said with a nod. Esther smiled, holding her breath, and Catherine flicked through the book and passed it over. 'I won't ask you for Absolution, but we'll say this prayer together after I've done it,' she said, pointing. 'You read the light writing and I'll join in when it's black.'

'I don't know if I—'

'Just words and they're only for me, nothing more unless you make it so,' she said.

'Just do it here?' Esther asked.

'They took away the confessional booth a while ago now. It's good enough here.'

As Esther took the book, Catherine went up to a silver tray near the altar, took something white and then knelt at the altar rail. Esther followed, sore on the stone. Catherine folded the white cloth between them on the lattice rail and then bent, hands clasped.

'Forgive me, Father, for I have sinned, it has been one week since my last confession,' and Esther went blank, no thoughts, just blank. She looked over to Catherine, whose thin hands were now placed together, her ring finger and thumbs bent. *I bet they're sore and she never says a thing about it.* Catherine was silent for a while, and Esther felt relieved that she wasn't going to confess out loud. Still, it made her feel vulnerable sitting next to her.

And then Catherine spoke. 'I'm sorry. I don't give you enough of a chance with me, too angry with you, and now too worried,' she said in a short tone. 'I worry and I know it's a sin and doesn't leave me with a clear head. I would sleep on the Mount of Olives, I know I would. I wear myself out with fear of you. I've never loved you, but John has and I follow him. He loved you. I don't make the best of what I have. I know it's a sin not to, and I have bitter thoughts sometimes. Too late for me now. Harold is getting worse and I'm afraid we're getting used to it like a slow frost. Not to be noticed till it bites. And these viruses are nothing but a worry without answers so people have gone quiet. We just get on. I try not to ask if you're with us, Lord. If you're watching. I try but never find more than a tight lip. As far as young Stephen is concerned. He works hard to help. I worry he's given up his rugby tournament. He's too young. No, he's too young.' There was a breathless silence for a moment. 'And then there's Esther.' Esther felt her back itch. This was a strange way to talk to her about things, if that's what was meant. 'Esther has a good heart, but she doesn't have you to lean on. And she doesn't have John. And what will she have when I'm gone?' She looked at Esther. 'If there was something I could give you I would,' she said, Esther quite still. 'Forgive me, Lord, I cleave to you from fear and not love. John had the love, but I never will. Always lost in Holy Week.' There was silence again and then she said, 'I give thanks for all the little things which keep us moving on, Amen.' She stayed there for a moment, Esther feeling clammy and closer to Catherine than she had ever been. It seemed sad to her now, sitting together like this, with the smell of polish.

And when Catherine turned to her with a sombre nod for her to read, Esther did without thinking, book held between them, their voices getting into a rhythm.

Man born of woman has but a short time to live,

We have our fill of sorrow,
We blossom like a flower and wither away,
We slip away like a shadow.
Holy God,
Holy and strong,
Holy and immortal,
Have mercy upon us.

Early the next morning Esther walked through the garden
and noticed she felt a sense of freedom. She went to the
allotment and started weeding the carrots, widening their
trough and stacking the sods in piles at the foot of the vege-
table patch. It had become nothing but bright yellow and
green netting with orange plastic buckets overturned and
wooden barriers to foxes, rabbits, stoats and anything else
that liked a carrot, bean or potato. She could taste the bitter
smell of cut grass and meaty soil; and then, without thinking,
she strode, hard-limbed, up to the netting and plastic tubs
and began to pull and twist them out with a crackling swish.
It shocked her, but as if building speed down a hill she flung
a bright orange bucket to the edge with a thud, and dragged
others, tangling and pulling along the line. Piling them into
a bright roll at the bottom.

'Too late,' she blew, out of breath, plunging her fork into
the soil, heaving with both hands clasped on the handle. The
earth giving way, small bulbs cracking at their stems. *Like
eggs*, she thought, *stayed in there all year like eggs.*

Fingers sore, some grazed, her vest soaking into her jumper,
she leant on the fork for breath and wiped wet hair from
her eyes. The soil looked like she felt: half-done, half-lived.

Then she turned to the lattice fence. It blocked her view. When she pressed her body against the slats it creaked and swayed, tight until it warped, split and crashed to the ground, struts sticking up like shards, sweet peas tangling, garden no longer half-seen. Wood and bundled colours dragged leaving ploughed lines to a pile at the gate. And then she raked the soil, thinking forcibly about something, not knowing what it was, jumper steaming, levering out plants and re-bedding them, working through the morning and past lunch until the garden widened to an oval, and then to the walls, grey clouds sitting as if they wouldn't move.

That evening she roasted a chicken and baked a large fruit-cake, laying it all on the table at once. When she sat, hot-cheeked, she felt surprised to see it there, almost as if someone else had made it. Catherine looked up at her every now and then. *Like a schoolmistress*, she thought.

'How's your rash?' she asked Harold at the dinner table.

'Oh, not so bad,' he answered, Esther noticing it was now up the side of his face and his eyes were red.

He smiled at her. 'Good spread this one tonight,' he said quietly, and she saw he was taking smaller mouthfuls than he used to. The opulence on the table next to his thin body made her feel bereft and defiant at the same time. Joe made his way through his plateful so fast he would need seconds soon. She looked at Stephen. 'Good day at school?' she asked.

'Oh aye,' he said. 'Maths wasn't a bother, but English was a bit strange. We had to write a news report on something local.'

'What did you write on?' Joe asked.

'Oh, just the auctions. It was the easiest.'

'Good lad!' Joe warbled. 'Give them what they need and have a life, eh?'

'Aye,' Stephen said, head down.

'Are you sure you would like to stop the rugby, Stephen? We can manage on a Saturday, you know,' Esther said, leaning forward.

'Oh aye, done now anyway, season's started. Joe and Dad are going to take me over the fells with a small flock, like they did in t'olden days.'

'You sure that's OK with the other farmers – the Landys and the Robinsons?'

'Aye, they'll be fine, Missus,' said Joe. 'We're over there looking for our sheep often enough and t'dogs know the ways. Nobody owns our fells. Be as it should be: "the good shepherd!"' he said with the gesture of holding a staff, making Stephen laugh and Catherine tut.

'Sounds good,' Esther said, smiling at Stephen.

'Aye,' he giggled.

'And teach him some of his grandfather's songs!' Harold said.

'Aye you'll be singing, we'll listen,' Stephen said, making Joe laugh.

'Room for more, if it's going,' Joe asked Esther.

'Help yourself,' she said, remembering that she would normally serve, but Joe just tucked in.

'Have you seen my penknife?' Harold asked.

'No, sorry, I haven't found it,' Esther said.

'You, Trin?' Catherine shook her head.

'No bother,' he said, looking frustrated.

'Where did you last use it?' Esther asked, knowing she'd asked before. She watched him think. Even his forehead was thinner.

'Nae bother,' he said. 'Joe's taken it, likely,' he laughed.

'Your penknife is nothing to mine,' Joe said, leaning to the side and pulling out a large wooden-handled knife with the blade tucked in.

'That's not mine,' Harold said.

'No, it isn't and you're not getting it, my man. It's a good'un, that is,' Joe chimed passing it to Stephen to look at.

Esther looked at the table for a moment. It felt all wrong. She shouldn't have made such a spread.

Harold looked at her. 'Have you seen my penknife?'

'No, Harold, I haven't,' she said, surprised by her frustration. He was becoming like her mother sometimes.

'No bother. It'll come around somewhere,' Joe said loudly and Harold nodded.

'It's not in the kitchen, Harold,' Catherine said. 'Is it George's one?'

'Aye.'

'Turn up somewhere.'

The following morning Esther was in the kitchen, trying to finish the cleaning before Catherine came in from scrubbing the porch steps again.

'My gran would have liked to go to church with you,' she said when Catherine came into the kitchen.

'She was friends with my sister, you know.'

'No, I didn't know.'

'Good friends until we lost her, our Sarah,' Catherine said, a light shake to her head.

'You never said you knew her well.'

'I didn't. She was about ten years older, but she was beautiful, I remember that and all her dried flowers.'

'Did she dry flowers, even when she was young?'

Catherine took a cloth and wiped the counter, her head to the side in thought.

'No, I think the flowers were later with your grandfather. We all left school earlier then, you know. You miss her.'

'Yes,' Esther said, disarmed. 'Miss the way she did things. Seemed a nicer life. Plain routine of things without her ways isn't enough somehow.'

'I have John. Always will. No better.'

'You're lucky with his letters.'

'Well,' she said, her voice becoming a little cheerful, 'what was that rhyme? But you have what she did. It's good enough for something. They live on with us if we let them. What was that rhyme?' Then she turned, cloth in hand, almost ceremonial, Esther thought and said, 'Ah yes.'

> 'Routine is life,
> Blessing is grace,
> The two together,
> Prevents haste.'

She looked down and smiled. 'One of Albert's,' she said.

Easter Sunday, Esther was up early. She found a parcel with her name on it in the kitchen. Brown paper, tied with a red ribbon. Inside were sheets of old rice paper, written on in fine, black ink. She opened it carefully.

Longtan Medical Centre
Central China
3rd March 1922

Dear Catherine,

May God bless and preserve you.

My happy news is that the gift of Mr Connolly and his engineering means that we now have the beginning of an electric generator. With Mr Connolly's expertise and my elbow grease we will be building it further with parts when they arrive from Yichang, which may mean next winter will be without illness from the cold. A gift indeed.

Just as in the Wesleyan meetings in Cockermouth, it is the Lord's work out here in the mountains, Catherine, but I admit to regular meditations on home. It is not the practice out here to observe life in Christ through such detail as we did, or rather the detail is found in hymns, Word and work. As life moves on, I realise we lived with the Lord in family ways that are rare even amongst fervent believers. I explained to Mrs Morrison that Mother would place a candle under a small statue of Mary for the Assumption, and that late on Christmas Eve the child who walked outside the longest with a lit candle had a special blessing, and it seemed far more Catholic in the recounting than in the living of it. So I left it there, not wanting to lose the grace of memories from the telling. If it is sentimental for a big man like me to dwell on these things and frame the days here with small offerings, then the Lord is in the sentiment. In those small rituals I am with you quicker than any letter could sail across the Indian Ocean and we 'dwell with Him'.

The work here continues and I often feel like quoting a piece of poetry I learnt when I was at school, 'My hairs are grey, but not with years', etc. No, with contractors and building. I am still working on the accommodation for doctors and assistants. As soon as the house is completed, then I will have to turn my attention to preparations for building the women's wing of our hospital. Others have tried to provide a mixed ward in the city, but even there it was not approved. Sit down with a clean sheet of paper, not even a plan, and you will realise what is embedded in the word 'preparations'. We are only waiting till the frost is over, when the actual preparations will commence.

I am pleased to give the news that Shu Hua, a bright young woman from Shanghai, is learning the routine of hospital work and will be visiting women in their homes with Mrs Murray until we are ready. While we wait, we are all working hard with the language and I am told my accent is a grave hindrance with enunciation. The patience of Mrs Murray is to be admired as I confess to enjoying a joke in her class stating that Chinese sounds closer to our farmers' talk than the Queen's English. However, it has been a great joy during the past few months to visit some of our nearer outstations, and take the Sunday service. The locals continue to humble the weariest of old men. No one could have desired a more attentive and, I might say, long-suffering audience, as they listened to me blundering through a sermon in Chinese far removed from Classic.

I will not say it is easy here, Catherine. The poverty continues to surprise, no matter how often it is seen, and the landowners can be merciless in their battle for power. But the Lord is never more full of heart than when there is labour to be done, and labour we are surely giving. Yesterday, Mrs Murray read through the early literature of the hospital, kept in the grand and efficient manner of an old box. The missionaries of Our Lord who came here in 1907 were brave and inspired. It took imagination to see a hospital where there were only small villages and mountains. What is new is often feared and it has taken time to gain trust. But a testament to that trust is our first patient brought here by his fellow monks. He had fallen in the mountains and for the five days he was with us, they camped beyond the precinct by the peach trees and drummed all day and all night. From the first day I offered them food, which they refused, choosing to fast until their brother recovered. Communication was attempted, but their dialect and mine were as if different languages. It was surely a loss of good tales to enter into from our different lives. By the third day, the staff were concerned by the sound, not only because it was disturbing sleep, including that of the patients but one lady began to

117

fear the drums. By the fourth day Mr Jackson, our visiting eye specialist, called a meeting about witchcraft, and consequently went down to the peach trees to attempt an explanation of the scientific medicinal route taken. He also talked about respecting each other's religion, including Christianity, which he stated did not believe in the medicine of drumming. They did not understand him and continued. Though I confess the drumming did begin to enter my thoughts, I admired their camaraderie and the ability to sit still while keeping a rhythm without exercise, food or sleep. Regrettably, on the fifth day the young monk died. I had the robe he arrived in washed, and in discussion with Mr Jackson, who wanted to ensure a Christian burial, we finally decided to bless him and carry him out to his brother monks, thinking they might want to take him to his family for the final rite. However, they circled his body in a low chant, bowed and left. Our bewildered Mr Jackson gave him a good funeral by the peach trees. I confess, Catherine, that I myself feel frustrated to have lived for a few days so near to these remarkable men and yet still know so little about them or their religion. But am very glad they would come here in a time of need. If Our Lord can reveal himself in a burning bush, my mind remains open to the forms and wonders of Christ.

I will pray for you and our family throughout Lent and into Easter. With that in mind, I have taken to brushing down the steps of the medical wing to greet everyone in the mornings. I am mindful that our rituals

do not always bring peace, Catherine, but with them
we are closer to Our Lord in pain as well as joy.

Ever yours,
John

Esther leant on the arm of the chair, thin paper in hand. What a life. She couldn't keep it, but to think that Catherine had wrapped it for her. How could she thank her? *Must read it again later, and get a map.*

The following Saturday she came down from her garden. She'd been planting some rhododendrons from the Manor, blue cornflowers and daffodils around the chair Catherine usually used. The closer she got to the yard, the more the sound of the metal gates clattering and sheep bleating took over. Second day of dipping. *It should be over by lunch*, she thought, puzzled by how she had taken against it over the last few years. Didn't want to be there when it happened. But Stephen was up in the dunking pen with Joe behind him, the ewe's legs scrattling on the metal plank, bulging eyes, trying to bounce out of the water, Stephen holding them under with a large pronged stick for the count of three, Ministry man sitting to the side, sleeves rolled up, pen and paper to hand. Tin of dip next to him in the sun. A sheep thrashed about and Stephen leant over with the look of his father and pressed his boot down into the dip with authority.

'Good lad,' crowed Joe, leaning forward to help if needed.

Harold was waiting behind to let the next one through,

while Clive was quietly working the other end of the yard, getting the sheep into the track.

'I'm about done, Harold. This young'n's tired me out. About time for a swap,' Joe said and Harold climbed up behind Stephen taking a mound of frightened wool, clinging to the bars on the narrow sides. One ewe kicked so fiercely they had to trap her in with a splash, Harold calling 'Come on old lady.' *It's hard work*, Esther thought, *but they seem to enjoy the challenge of it*

In the afternoon Esther sat on the porch step, Catherine's cloth nailed to the wall beside her. Dipping was over but the metal bones of it were yet to be cleared away. She listened to Stephen and his friends running around playing tag, she knew it would make her late for her mother, but wanted to watch them for a while, feel their sound marking the yard, ducking around the dipping gates. She'd have liked to watch the young lads tuck into the cake, but she set off with no wave from Stephen, so caught in his game.

VII

Spring 1987

Harold

Rain lathered onto the fells, clinging to the clouds like froth.
Matted moss and grass lifted its weave to let the waters gully
through underneath; light flickering the hidden streams
across the fell like a miner's lamp seen here and there. Rust
on the juniper tree painted its bark with streaks of ochre,
and on the other side of Ard water pushed down the flanks,
almost in a wide flat wave to the beck. And when it reached
the banks, it spilt, clear and determined into the tide, spreading its threads, cleansing so deep into the skin of things it
flattened and twisted long yarns before prising them loose,
surrendered, gulping over stones towards the lake.

Some sheep were caught in the water, their stippled wool
and shaggy tails pulling them into the current, legs tucked
under like a buoy, a look of nonchalance on their faces, until
one rang out like a bell, and the rest joined in the chorus.

Harold was on his way downstream, Stephen in place
above waiting, collar up, glaring under the pouring water. As
soon as Harold was ready he watched, his right eye always
swollen and hardly working now, but he could still see

Stephen in the fresh torrent, young legs firm and spread amidst the rocks, flow spraying his thighs, looking downstream. He grabbed a sheep and tillered it past the small waterfall and watched as it floated down, turning slightly in an eddy, his light blue eyes pierced, rooted, waiting for the sheep to get to his father where the waters slowed. *Just eleven but tall and strong, like Albert*, Harold thought. Once the sheep were clear and checked, Stephen made Harold laugh by standing in the rain on one foot and pouring out the water from his wellies before they walked home, clouds charcoal dark, Hemp at their side.

Harold's leg was twitching by the time he got back. Not his regular shudder every now and then, but a steady twitch. Once he'd bathed and was about to pull his trousers on, he watched it. *Mind of its own.* He was used to hiding his hands when they quivered, but this was strange, could hardly feel it. *Be gone soon*, he decided and went down to supper. Joe was waiting at the table, wet through but refusing a bath, as usual.

'Get this dry jumper on, Joe. It's yours,' Esther said.

'Not bothered, thank you.'

'You're getting worse, Joe. We've always got things of yours here just for this.'

'Aye well as may be, but not bothered, thank you.'

'Like an old man!'

Joe gave Esther an annoyed look, so Harold strode to the table and sat opposite.

'All right, Joe?'

'Aye.'

Harold nodded at Esther, who folded the jumper and left

it on one of the comfy chairs by the fire and went to the kitchen.

'Any finds?' he asked.

'No, all clear. Bloody Millie's eye's gone, though, bled into.'

'The left one?'

'Aye,' Joe said, knocking the table leg in a stretch.

'Sorry to hear that, Joe. She's been a good'un, that.'

Joe didn't answer, fiddling with his fork. 'Thinking on going with her,' he said.

'What do you mean?'

'Packing it in when she goes.'

Harold held the table to keep his hands steady. 'Thou diven't mean that, Joe?'

'Well, no dignity in it any more. A man's not his own.'

'Not his own?'

'Aye. Ministry men have it now, sending in the "experts" . . . changing their minds. Lost the milkers to the tankers; fells to the registers; seasons to the subsidies and markets to the tills. Have to stand by and watch our ways pass by. Might be better, but it's not for me. It's one size fits all, it's all numbers. And what do we have to show for it? Food mountains. Food bloody mountains sold off cheap and funnily enough no more guarantees for our price. But they've no responsibility, we've just suddenly got to stop the production they changed our lives to make. And not just stop, some will be fined for it.' Harold looked confused. 'Yes, if they produce their normal quota they'll be fined, because now the powers that be have decided it's too much. And we won't mention the pathetic show of butter vouchers for the pensioners.

Sorry, I'm full bellied with it, Harold, not fit for company, I know that. Time to move on or I'll turn into a bitter man. Falklands took over and Thatcher's in for keeps. I've not the guts for farming for them.'

'Been to too many of them meetings, Joe,' Harold said weakly. 'It's the way it's gone, that's all. Have to sit tight. Rein in, done it before.'

'You're right, lad. It's not pretty, but I've lost. I've no patience left in me to wait.'

'What will you do?'

'Stephen!' Esther called up the stairs before she came in with a tatie pot.

'Join in the workers' party for a while. Best way to vent.'

Esther sat down, only to pop up and call at the bottom of the stairs. When she sat again, she looked worried.

'New regulations?' she asked.

'No, well,' Harold said, not wanting to explain, hoping it would turn into one of Joe's rants, rather than this. 'What have they been saying in those meetings, then?' he asked, trying to get Joe to talk.

'It's not the bloody meetings, it's me, lad. I've lost the stomach for it, I'm sorry lad, it's good for you, I know it is.'

'For what? Fells the same, we're the same. For what? You're just letting them change what you see and it's no different.'

'It is, lad. No dignity in it, and that's all we've got in the end. Not saying you're not doing well. You're the best of them.'

Harold felt his chest bursting. His hands gripping his thighs under the table. Joe was right. Their finances had got worse. Increasing the flock helped a little but they'd never recovered from two bad winters in a row. The prices were going down and the drainage allowance had just been cancelled for his bottom field, which needed regular help. He had no idea how they would make ends meet.

'Years of work, years of building the flock,' Joe said, looking up to Harold from under a furrowed brow. 'I'm sorry lad, I've no faith in the Ministry but I've faith in you. You'll survive.' He looked at the table. 'Den of thieves,' he muttered under his breath.

Catherine came in, followed by Stephen, who sat down, looked around the table and said 'All right? Summat happened?'

'You really thinking on leaving, Joe?' Esther asked quietly.

Stephen gasped. 'What you want to do that for?'

Joe sat back with a breath trying to change his tone. 'It's time you took over, lad,' he said with a little warmth. 'It's your show now. About time I fettled off and made a patch of my own.'

Stephen stared, fork gripped in his fist.

'Be around and about, of course,' Joe said. 'Still go up t'fells with a small flock for a weekend. Never get rid of me.'

'It's come as a bit of a shock, Joe,' Esther said, leaning forward to serve. 'You'll be missed.'

Harold looked over to Catherine who sat calmly. Seemed like she knew.

'How long you been thinking on it?' Harold asked.

'About a year now. Not saying till I was sure. But we've bad times, you can't walk the lanes without another farm for sale,' he flicked a look to Catherine. 'No, I've no peace on the fells now. Sorry to say it, but they've scarred the land for me. Ownership. Worse than stripping the forests.'

'What you mean?' asked Stephen.

'Up to your father now to find new ways in farming. He can move with the times. I'm old school.'

'Old school?'

'Aye, when you stand equal with any other man and let the land take you her way. They've started to see the damage of their greed on the fells and look at conservation subsidies, but. It's the thin end of the wedge. They'll not take responsibility for the fall.'

'That right, Dad?'

'Well, yes, I'd say some of it, but nothing marks the fells for long. Can never be owned, not really. People think they do, but. More powerful than the rest of us put together. Just takes a harsh winter to show who's boss up there.'

'Aye, you'll be right,' Joe said looking at Stephen, who'd put his fork down and sunk in his chair. 'Listen to your father now. He's the better man.'

Harold sat into the evening by the fire, the rash on his temple itching, making his bad eye twitch, his hands quaking even when they were relaxed. Without Joe, they were one down and needed another man. Stephen could do more, but it wasn't enough. He tried to get his mind to think it through step by step, but the shock of it seemed to blank him. Joe'd always been there. Wasn't right without him. Catherine came through in her old grey slippers, a shawl wrapped over her dressing gown, carrying two mugs of tea.

'You up, Trin? Must be about midnight.'

126

'Couldn't sleep,' she said, putting his mug down and sitting in the other chair.

'Not be much sleep here tonight.' He looked over. 'Didn't see it coming, that one. Was always talking, but I thought it was just Joe. Should have listened more.' He turned back to the fire, glad she was there, and they sat in silence for a while and then he said 'You didn't look too surprised, mind,' and they were silent again for a while before she said, 'Needs to make his own way.'

'We are his own way. It's as much his farm as anyone's.'

'Soon be Stephen's,' she said.

'Aye, that's true, but he'll need us here to support him. And Joe's part of it.'

'He is, but son, he's not been happy.'

'No, you're right. I see that, but we get through. Good enough is the best we have mostly. Bloody politics. Sorry, Trin, but . . .' He tried to think of the fell without Joe. 'He'll have to stay in the cottage, of course.'

'I think he's planning for Cockermouth,' she said, taking another sip of her tea.

Harold thought of Joe's cottage, bare-wall empty. He didn't have much, a few magazines and a grandfather clock, but what he had belonged there.

'No,' he said slowly. 'He can't just walk away with nothing for it. I'll have to give him part of the herd.' A log cracked and fell charred into the orange heat. *He'll not want it*, he thought.

'Well, he can do what he likes with it,' he said with his heart welling up. 'But I'll not let him go with nothing to his name. That I will not do.'

*

'Come on, lad!' Harold shouted, impatiently pacing the hall. His legs were aching but he wasn't going to notice that, not today. 'Come on!' he called again.

'He'll be down in a minute,' Esther said. 'Don't push too hard, now.'

'I won't, love, but we'll miss the first bets.'

'He'll be down soon, only just got in,' Esther said, kissing him on the cheek. 'You look good,' she said.

'Always beautiful,' he said, touching her cheek in return, seeing his hand shake and stepping back to notice he was fevering a little, then roused to the sound of Stephen bounding down the stairs. 'Come on lad, let's be off,' he said, Stephen nodding, cantering out past him, while Harold wiped his top lip to kiss Esther on the cheek and followed on.

'I'll drive,' Stephen said.

'No, you will not!'

'No different from the tractor.'

'It may not be in your eyes,' Harold said, getting into the driver's seat, 'but it is in Bobby's eyes and that's what counts.'

'They'd never know.'

'If you drive up to the hound trails they will!'

Once they were there, Harold loved the sound of it, taking over a field with haggling for a bet, lines of men waiting, counting their change. Yelps of hounds hungry for scent. The runner set off trailing aniseed and soon everyone stood in line, caps down, eyes pierced to the fell talking to their hounds, holding their wailing bodies back, until the whistle blew and they fired out to a roar of bidding 'Go on, go on there lad!' each with his own call. And then, between news from the tops, they would shout 'What you got a ticket on?'

All capped in tweed, all gritted with the fells and feeling the freedom of it. Parting like waves for the young lad. 'Oh, this young Stephen? Good young man in him now,' they'd say to Harold. 'Take over the farm next, will you?' they'd shout and when Stephen said 'Aye,' they folded him in with a cheer, patting his back. 'Harold's got one'll be taking it on,' they called like a favoured bet. Harold so proud he could've grown feathers.

That night there was a blue light in his room as he prised the window open, curtains not closed. He stretched through his cramps carefully, so he didn't wake Esther. He'd walk down to Joe's early to meet him and they could take the fells in together while they talked it through. No matter how hard things were, he'd offer him what he deserved: half the herd, fell-grazing rights and fields, and of course wages, including the normal rent for his cottage until his first crop of lambs, and then they could help each other on their way, two farms together. It was the right thing to do. Joe could farm his own way and they'd sort through things like they always did. He felt ashamed he hadn't thought of that a few years earlier. Took Joe for granted. Forgot he was a man with his own life to build. And Joe was right, they'd lost their way, their principles, the reason why they were all doing this, the land, the old way of life, and from now on he would put it right.

When he got to Joe's the morning hadn't yet risen from the ground and frost was lifting splinters from the door. He could hear Joe inside and wondered if he should wait, but he felt the good news overtake him and banged with the side of his fist.

'Harold, early day got you?'

'Aye,' he said, striding in to the smell of coffee.

'Have a cup?'

'Aye,' he said again, as he sat on the chair to the far side of the small table from the cooker.

Joe filled another mug of coffee, Millie pacing at his heels, thumped it on the table alongside the milk bottle and sat, Millie's snout soon on his lap.

'Not far to go now to the markets,' he said, clearing his throat.

'No, not long now,' Harold said, and thought he'd wait till they were on the fells. Best to walk alongside a man when you have news.

'Be tough this year, mind.'

'Aye, but I think it'll work out. Might take a couple of years, but we'll put it right in the end.'

'Credit due, lad. You've always a plan or two.'

'Aye, getting there!' he said with a smile, as Joe looked down.

'Now then, that is good news.'

'Aye, well, it'll be hard going likely, but best things are.'

'They are that,' Joe said, a mouth full of bread.

When they were on the fells Harold walked with Joe at his side, digging into the ground as if his stride went below the soil. Harold's rhythm had changed over the years, smaller steps, earth drawing him to a standstill, and the alternating pace of them both and the wind blowing against him in different directions made his dizziness worse.

As they neared the peak, he let Joe go ahead and watched the back of his boots, steadying himself. At the top he wondered if they should sit for a moment, but when he called to Joe, the wind took his words and he realised he would have to wait till they were over the brow to be heard. And as they walked, the valley, almost still, cupped them side by side, the beck as calm as glass.

'It's a plan should have been made a good few years ago, Joe, and I'm sorry for that,' he said. He could feel his chest almost fold with guilt. *If it weren't for the plan, I'd have no life left in me*, he thought.

'Oh, now, we're past that, Harold. Nobody's fault the way things are now.'

'No, but things should have been done.'

'Aye lad, that's for sure,' Joe said, striding ahead. Harold working to keep up.

'Well, I've been and seen it now, too late mind, but that's it.'

'Be glad to look at it for you if it helps.'

'Aye, well,' he felt out of breath and stopped, his chest pounding.

Joe turned. 'You OK, lad?'

'Aye,' he said, with such a joy in his heart he felt he could hardly see. 'Aye, Joe, but I'm sorry it wasn't yours earlier, should have been, but we got swept away with the years.'

'What you talking about, lad?'

'The farm, Joe, it's yours. Well, half of it. You have half the herd, the grazing rights, the field. We can share the hay and yours is the cottage and we'll have it sorted till you've had your first year's crop. More, we'll pay it together, for as long as you need to get it set in your own way, Joe. Your own farm. It's only right.' He watched Joe, waiting for him to be home again, like the family they were, almost brothers, working together, watching each other, waiting.

'Harold, lad,' Joe said, eventually, a redness coming into his face, a gloss to his eye. 'They threw away the mould with you and none will say different.'

Harold took a step forward, up the hill, waiting for the moment. Joe looked down at him and smiled, the peak raised behind him. 'I don't know what to say, lad. I didn't expect it, but now I see you, I should have known it. No one would have thought of that except you.'

'It's right, Joe.'

'In our hearts it's right, lad, and I'll never forget it. A new mark in this valley, if ever there was one. But lad, I'm sorry, I can't take it,' he said, wet cheeked.

'Why not, Joe?' he said. 'It's right. I should have done it earlier. I'm sorry for that.'

'No, lad, never earlier and never now. It's not to be parted, it's for Stephen to take on and make a life, and there's Esther to look after and Catherine.'

'Please, Joe,' he said, feeling his throat thinning. 'You belong here,' he tried to say.

'Never a better man than you,' Joe said. 'Like your father, but you're not going to let me go unless I tell you it all. May be right. Thought best not to and hope you'll forgive me that, but we'll have it said the once and never mention it again,' he said, looking larger somehow, chestnut brown eyes above him on the fell. 'You'll lose the farm if you're not careful, lad. You're a good worker, never a doubt, but you can't do the day you used to, Harold, and best not, otherwise you might tire yourself out. But that's not the way for the young lad. He needs his father. The rent of my cottage and the wage for me is too much.' Harold struggled to talk, but Joe stopped him with his hand. 'Fair's fair, I'll have my say. If your father were here, he'd say it was the best thing to do for you, lad. Our income is the same as the income for one of the lowland farm tractor drivers. Take my rent and wages and get one hand who lives local when you need it, contract in for clipping and hay time and make a plan to pay off the loans with the rest.' Harold struggled to speak again. 'It's none better, Harold. I've seen the books and you're going to run at a loss this year again, no doubt.'

Harold struggled to breathe, felt his body drain. 'You can't go, Joe,' he said.

'I have to, lad. I couldn't stay for my own good and watch you go down. Not got it in me. And we'd all be down in the end, no good till any of us that,' he said, his chest seeming broader, his voice strong.

'We'd work it out,' Harold spat, holding in his sobs.

'Aye, that's what we have,' Joe said, his voice now filling Harold's ears as if it were in the valley. 'And I want it all for you, lad. You'll not lose it, not now. George'd never forgive me. It's best thing for the farm,' he said, the light streaking behind him, his face becoming shadowed. He stopped for a moment. 'Always be here for you, lad, always solid that.'

In the afternoon Harold forgot his chores and went up to the garden to find Esther, but she wasn't there. He sat on the bench he'd made with Joe, looking out over the two circles of roses. A raven flew past, seemed too close. He felt wrung out, as if his body were bruised, hands twitching, even when he pressed them under his thighs. They'd have Joe for a year. *He'd give that if he was asked.* On the fell with him one more season. Be a hard year, but they needed him till they could work it out. He had to think it through again, but couldn't, just couldn't . . . not today. He had nothing left.

He must have fallen asleep for a while, because when Esther woke him his arms were numb and he took a while to steady himself on his feet, his damned knees playing up, as they walked back down the hill. He thought she would scold him, saying he could catch a chill like that, but she was silent by his side, arm linked in his and he was grateful for it.

Back by the fire, Stephen sat listening to the radio, another football match on, the commentator raising his voice to a near-goal. He looked pale, Harold thought, growing quicker than he could feed and his hand was bandaged.

'What you do with the hand, lad?'

'Oh, bloody tractor engine.'

'Nasty?'

'Aye, but it'll do.'

'Make sure and bathe it now.'

'Aye, Mam's on that.'

'Right.'

'When you do it?'

'This morning.'

'All right?'

'Aye, it'll sort. You all right?' he said.

'Oh, aye,' Harold answered, trying to sound relaxed,

though his legs were cramping till they warmed up. 'Your mother's done such a good job on that garden, I fell asleep in it!'

Stephen laughed. 'We were out looking for you in the fells.'

'On the fells?'

'Aye, Joe's just gone home, like, but we weren't sure where you'd got to.'

'What you all do that for?'

'Joe said you should have been back hours ago and Hemp was whining about the yard, so we thought you'd maybe had a fall.'

'What a lot of fuss, I was asleep. Well now ...' Harold said, embarrassed. 'Should have checked the garden!'

'Aye,' Stephen laughed, another near-goal coming through.

VIII

Spring 1990

Catherine

Catherine held the bible out towards Harold, hovering for a while, and then placed it back on her knee, pale pink apron fluttering slightly at the hem.

'Harold?' she called, but he didn't turn. 'Harold?' she tried in a higher song and still he didn't turn. Maybe he was thinking about things as he levelled the slabs, mud dug and shaken, a strong focus to the side of his face. His dark hair was stuck in the shape of his cap which now hung out of his pocket. 'Scissors out next week,' she said.

Snowdrops spread across the lawn, as if a stream had come through. *Our Lady reminding us of winter*, she thought. *Hope of Christmas in spring.* She picked up the bible and opened to the marked page. She had her mother's hands now, bent swollen knuckles, especially her thumbs. As she looked up, Harold stood back to check the path and she wondered if his chest was still sore. She waited for a moment to see if he would glance over, but he set to again. *Just leave him to it, bit of time to himself.*

The Bible passage had the comfort of an old friend, and

the Good Friday theme a reproach from within a family. She licked her fingers to turn the thin page and, as she leant close to read, her lips soon pursed.

'No use being lazy, Catherine,' she said.

And, as if the movement in the garden and the stone wall behind it clicked into a stage set, she saw John walking towards her.

'Never the same reading if you let the words in.'

She nodded, pulled a breath into her chest and read on, 'never easy,' she whispered leaning forward again with more focus and read out loud. 'For he shall grow up before him as a tender plant, and as a root out of a dry ground: he hath no form nor comeliness ... He is despised and rejected of men; a man of sorrows, and acquainted with grief: and we hid as it were, our faces from him.' She looked over the words again as if they were a landscape. 'You're either with him in your sorrows or against him in your sin,' John would say. He would admit to both. Catherine knew she was both. Mostly sin. Tired of trying to pray. And for a moment it was as if John touched the back of her hand and she saw her mother's prayer beads. 'I'm weary, lad,' she mumbled.

'Take one line and repeat it,' she heard.

She looked over the page. 'For he shall grow up before him as a tender plant.' *That might be nice to read a few times*, she thought. Then the phrase '*All we like sheep have gone astray*' caught her sight and as she repeated it for the fourth and fifth time, she slowly felt gathered and innocently happy to be penned into the walled garden, which became an old field in which, for a moment, she had nothing to do but belong.

*

Later, she passed the porch and checked the rag she'd hung the Saturday before, rain and early mornings crinkling it, matting the stains. Esther came out.

'Lazarus Saturday?' she asked.

Catherine nodded.

'If it's not too late, I'd like to do one this year,' she said.

Catherine looked almost past her eyes for something.

Esther blushed.

'It's Good Friday already,' she said.

'Oh, I know. Probably too late for this year.'

Nothing wrong with doing it again. 'Aye, Lazarus and Good Friday working together,' she said and walked in to get one of the old cloths from the pantry, neatly spreading it out on the kitchen top for Esther to look at; holes and washed stains through it like honeycomb. And then, she began to rip where the edge was frayed; tugging the cotton, squeezing her sore fingers to keep hold of the tear, appreciating Esther not trying to help. Once it was in three strips, she gave one to Esther. 'For under your sheet,' she said, 'until tomorrow.' She took the second for herself and the third was put into a bowl in wait.

By late morning most things were baked and prepared for the next two days; least done the better on Easter weekend. In the afternoon Catherine walked up to the garden gate, wellingtons rasping the ground. Her feet were getting smaller but socks helped, and the sound had become a rhythm to walk to. Through the gate, the grass seemed sloped. *My eyes again.* The oak trees spread grey. 'They'll be budded,' she murmured as she walked over the grass, which seemed to have become lumpy as the years went by and when she got to the tree, she examined the lower branches. The waxed buds shone tight, and for a moment she heard voices, distant conversations in the garden. They settled her in familiar sounds.

'Trin, you happy with this?'

She started.

'You all right, Grandma?'

Harold and Stephen stood in the middle of the garden, not far away at all. She looked at them and then walked determinedly over. Being near them seemed to make her stride out, though the wellies couldn't always keep up.

'Oh yes, very good. Bit wide, mind, but very good.'

'Wide?'

She nodded, but stood appreciating the path which now stretched from the gate to the bench. 'No, it's good, that's it,' she said, noticing they were standing in a line as if at the dog trials waiting for judgement. 'Good.' She bent to clear a few twigs alongside it. Not so easy to bend her knees now and her back would make her topple if she didn't, so she left it at that, noticing that Harold and Stephen had joined in.

In the evening she walked up Newlands path to church with Harold. The wind blew her old hat around her ears. She thought she could hear the brook amidst the sound of the felt and concentrated her sights on the top of the hill. When Esther drew up in the car, Catherine kept walking. She knew they were waiting for her, slow as she was, but she wanted to walk further. When she did get in the car, she kept her eyes on the road and later went ahead of them up the steps to the church, holding the church door to steady herself before she went in.

The vigil had started, but the new vicar still made a point of coming over full of smiles, greeting them loudly at the bible table which had been taken over by empty coffee cups and plates of Rich Tea biscuits. He let them know they could get refreshments any time throughout the evening if needed, even showed them to a pew. Catherine nearly sat in it, but at the last minute decided to go to her old place, even if it was ill-mannered.

Candles were lit on the altar. It had been prepared before the service. Heavy velvet and linen folded away leaving bare slate. A cross stood at the centre but there was no monstrance. It had been polished, wrapped in paper and put in a trunk a few years ago. The statues were bare, unveiled, watching. They seemed stern, even panicked at the sight. She sat back, comfortably settling into the pew, which now engulfed her, pleased her hearing wasn't so good. The intermittent readings of the seven last words with homilies wouldn't be such a distraction. 'No matter,' she whispered, *if it serves the younger ones. Maundy Thursday and Good Friday in one.* But there was no real sense of waiting in them, no hard cold floor to remind them of life, what with the talks and hot tea. *Be stuck when it hits them later. Life doesn't stop for suffering. But there's waiting in it if you're the one in trouble. John would have done it right. He would have waited in the dust of the desert, never moving until the Lord found him.* But the day before she hadn't gone to the garden. All she had done for Maundy Thursday this year was sit under the juniper tree, wind almost blowing through her nowadays. She'd even felt a moment of warmth as if Albert were there. It stayed with her all evening. She was too tired for Gethsemane, too old. 'Done my living,' she said. 'No teaching me how to cleave now. Always scolded at dawn.'

She put her bible on the shelf in front and looked up to the altar. The wooden lid of the small stone baptismal font next to it looked as if it wasn't on properly. *They'll not know its eight corners are for Holy Week. Forgotten.* She rested back in her pew. *Well, may as well be forgotten if it's no use to them.* The stone of the altar settled her, took her outside to the fells for a moment and then back into the church. 'Altar's been here longer than the rest of us,' she mumbled in the dull quiet. Always sadness in her these days once she settled. Soon breathing as if in sleep. 'Not easy,' she whispered and tried to look at the stone again. *Daren't.* But, for a moment the altar had a mind of its own, drawing her in, peering as someone looks through trees to the land on the other side. *Yes*, she thought, nodding. *He's right, my time soon, age unlocking me like an old key.* She felt strength from admitting it, hand pushed on the bible to straighten her back. *I've fear*, she thought with determination, as if staring at the altar now kept fear around the edge of her sight. *Couldn't see it crack, no, couldn't see it*, she thought, feeling she would break if the altar did. *But I'll look Him in the eye when it's my time.* 'I'll look at Him then,' she said fiercely. And, back sore, she sank into the pew, tired against the wood.

*

That night after the vigil she took out a soft purse with pieces of juniper bark from a necklace John sent her, the thread thin and broken in parts. They felt good in her hand. Almost like rosary beads. And she pulled out one of his letters from near the bottom of a pile.

Longtan Medical Centre
Central China
27th June 1928

Dear Catherine,

We are working hard to defend the hospital from the hands of bandits, rebels and troops alike. While you may have heard by now that Mrs Murray and Mrs White have been under siege in Wuhan, others have managed to get to Shanghai and I believe they found a boat that will take them to Europe if not home. I expect you are aware that some missionaries have been taken captive. I only address it, Catherine, to make sure your concern is rested. I must insist that you remember I am a man of the mountains and have the benefit of long winter tracking. Mr Connolly and I will remain for a while but be in no doubt: for two oxen, we are both canny men.

I will send this letter with Thomas, as he is to travel to Shanghai, but it may be some time before I am able to send you another letter, so please remember what I have said. If I give thanks for anything it is for the fervent following of Our Lord's teaching and the chance to serve. I am glad I came. Thankfully we've employed locals for a while and it is they who will now stay with the sick and wounded without their very presence posing the risk that ours would. You may have heard that the hospital in Changsha has been burned because foreigners were still living there. With that in mind, we prepare. The patients are certainly not fit for travel.

We turn to the Lord in these times, Catherine, and if we have the stomach for truth, we are sure to see that the love of God does not make life easier. There's no wisdom to be found in cruelty to good families in the villages, or the hunger and desperation of soldiers. On these things faith sheds no light. If anything, it simply keeps one in line. Some have held on to hope, imagining another world in place of this one. They pray fervently for that world to arrive. It is my prayer also that we all live in a peaceful community together, but I know that prayer cannot will it to happen. I left that hope behind with the war. Good people are surrounded by earthquakes, bandits and desperate troops. I can only pray God's Will is done and for the courage to keep moving forward and not sink with the ship. I can't say I have cared for the harsh attitude I have found in the distribution of wealth or the politics here, but I can say, Catherine, with a dear heart, that I care about these people and maybe that is an Eden of its own, an island in a storm. It is against my nature to leave anyone in times of trouble, but so be it. As foreigners, we've become the source of danger to the very people we serve. Their hope is now in running the hospital for all

143

sides to heal anyone, including soldiers. Mr Connolly and I are clearing all residences of any trace of foreign living, so that there will be rooms available for soldiers or bandits away from the patients, and we are storing supplies in different hiding places, so that they will be able to withstand the raids. We work to the last moment for their safety.

Dearest Catherine,

Thomas is to leave for Shanghai early, so I will end this letter now, asking you to trust in me and not worry. If I don't make it down to Shanghai myself, I will have helped to the last minute and escaped with a good store to hide in the mountains – and you know as well as I do that the mountains can be my home and refuge for years. If you don't hear from me, be sure in the knowledge that I am well, but making contact will give away my position. I may even get the chance to visit the Sichuan Mountains, which have such height I expect to find the scent of our Skiddaw, Helvellyn or Scafell Pyke in their peaks. I've heard there is a monastery hidden somewhere there from before the birth of Our Lord. Some years ago, I had a desire to seek it out and if I am to become a traveller, it may be my time. I should be away from trouble Catherine, but if not, I have gone as willingly as any man with a desire to find some answers from my maker. If there is no burning bush in the mountains, there will be a burning heart.

'Love divine, all loves excelling,
Joy of heaven, to earth come down;
Fix in us thy humble dwelling,
All thy faithful mercies crown.

May the Lord bless you and all our family, dear Catherine,
and guide us into His everlasting light. Amen.

Ever yours,
John

She leant back for a while and then, as if stirring out of sleep, she turned to put it back in the suitcase and saw Albert's old bible. Thin paper folded into its pages. A flicker of horror passed across her face. She'd not read those letters since George died. Couldn't. Memory of the shoebox in his room for 'the war letters' too strong. Evenings of George quietly rereading them. Her betrayal of his final wishes so fresh she might have just done it. And she couldn't pass them on to Harold or Stephen telling them that they were some of the letters promised to be buried with George. That she hadn't been able to part with all John's war letters, not even for her own son. Hidden in a bible, of all places. She sat in the cold room. Grey light. 'I'm ready to go,' she said in disgust. 'Love and betrayal stain you in this life. Neither one more than the other.'

Early the next morning she took the cotton rag from under her sheet and had to pull the sides to pierce it onto the old nail in the porch. The new rag hung on top of the stained one. Seemed unnaturally flat and clean.

Esther found her checking the tins in the kitchen.

'Shall I put mine in the porch, Catherine, or I was remembering, I think some time ago you told me about John tying his to a tree, that right?'

'Aye,' she said, surprised at Esther's memory of it.

'Well, I thought I might walk up to the garden and tie it there. Come with me?'

Catherine nodded and after closing the biscuit tins, she slipped the third rag into her pocket and they walked up, silver light bringing out the water in dark grasses. She watched as Esther tied her cloth to a branch of the old oak tree and then they stood back for a while.

'Why do you sleep on it?' Esther asked.

'Wouldn't know, really.'

Esther still looking up.

'They say you tie it up so he's not a stranger when he comes,' Catherine added.

'But why from your bed?'

'Different kind of sleep till the one we think it is.'

'We think it is?'

'Aye, sleep of Lazarus. We never know what that is.'

Esther kept watching the branch.

'A hard week Holy Week and you'd be forgiven for empty dreams on the Saturday. Or dark thoughts.' Catherine tried to remember what she'd been taught. 'They say we're calling to Christ on the Saturday. For him. It's an empty day of him. The only day empty of him; being as he's in the tomb. And they say we hang the cloth to show he will come to us tomorrow. Take us with him, out of our tomb like Lazarus. We've to show faith in the Sunday. Like a balm,' she said,

146

her voice thinning, squeezing the cloth in her pocket. 'Even Our Lord can't cheat death before Sunday,' she said in John's words as she looked up at the white rag. And she stepped forward, noticing Esther's surprise as she unravelled the third rag, surprising herself as she felt John's neck bend to her. And, arms shaking at the height, she tied it around him, taken by the bow of his head, the dirt on his hands and how peaceful he was.

After a while she looked over at Esther, wondering what she had seen, not wanting to ask. Esther looked up, clear-eyed, and together they walked back in silence. Halfway down the path Esther asked something and she knew she'd looked blank. *Wasn't just dirt on his hands, they were scarred,* she thought. *But he was peaceful in the garden.*

IX

Winter 1993

Harold

It was a white day. The horizon was matted with beech and oaks, still bare from winter, still black with hidden sap.

'Soon to bud, though you've only the memory of it yet,' Harold muttered.

He looked over his shoulder, his right eye now a murky blur, and paced up through Knott Rigg, earth nearly dug into steps the further he climbed. Light filled the fields like frost. It snowed his sight. The fever would come and go, but the pressure in his bad eye was constant, the other eye streaking colours into the sides of his thoughts like lanterns at night. His chest heaved with the climb, the force of it made him feel stronger and pressed against him like fierce company.

'Drink in the day and suck up the rains,' he whispered, looking down to gnarls of grass for safety, measuring his balance. 'Where's that blooming dog?' he growled, bracing himself to look out.

The light pierced like metal again and he whistled, squinting along the fells to see movement, but found none. He thought for a moment. Saw himself set out, check the hay and tighten the ropes. He felt his left hand, scraped from the yarn, right hand now clawed but still able to grip, yes, he'd tightened the ropes and then come up here.

Where is that damned mutt? He thought of the vales and gullies he knew along the fell. *She found something?* He waited for a moment. 'Should know better than to ignore a call,' he said with a bite.

The wind blew round his knees and under the heather, rumbling the twists of bleached grey, so buoyant in clusters it seemed to be searching beneath. 'No point without her, lad,' he said to himself, as if his father spoke. 'No, you've to ... I haven't gone and left her in the yard, have I?' He whistled again. Could he hear barking down in the farm? No. 'Best gan and see, lad,' his father would say. 'Aye,' he replied, obedient, and began his descent, used to watching his unsteady pace on the steep tread, a sudden flash of anger coming over him and then passing like wind into obedience again. 'Damned collywobbles!' He was relieved when he got down to the bracken, filling the space round his thighs, keeping him straight.

And there it was, her sound towards the juniper tree, rushing through the bracken, hissing through like sheen, her black snout and shaggy low canter clipping round sections, parting the russet fronds towards Harold. He dropped to the ground in wait, in relief at the sound, and Matty swept in, her itchy silk to his face and a warm belly to his hands.

'There now, lass,' he soothed. 'What you been doing there?' Her tongue was warm on his chin. 'Enough of that you daft mottle,' he said, pushing her snout away. 'What's at the juniper? Got a find? Summat to show me, eh?' She paddled around him, clearly not pulling him away to anything. 'Well

149

there now, Matilda, it's a mystery, but here you are,' he said lying back, stroking her, the smell of cold soil around them, the thin grass before spring.

'Matty!' Stephen's voice bellowed out nearby.

Harold bolted upright, staggering to stand. 'You buggered the lot out of me. What you doing here?' Stephen looked up to him. 'Not feedin' the back lot?'

'Aye,' Stephen said, pale-faced, as if he had asked a question.

Harold stood confused. 'What you doing here, lad?' he said again, the tail end of his words quietening as he looked down to steady himself, feeling the very gesture of looking down made him guilty of something.

'No bother, Dad. Just thought you'd want Matty with you for scourin'.' His son flushed as he spoke. 'You'd left her in the farm on t'chain, Dad, not loosened her off yet. But it's no bother, easy done.'

Harold stopped for a moment, unsure of how to take it in.

'No,' he said and bit his lip. 'Not easy done, lad,' avoiding Stephen's face, guiding his sight over the bracken. 'Just damned stupid.' He took a breath, a flash of anger forcing his eyes to the light, like a strike. 'Aye well, thanks, lad, no bother,' he called, staying where he was, feeling the rope mark on his hands. 'Right you are, son,' he said, pulling out an old, crinkled handkerchief to wipe the back of his neck.

'Righto,' Stephen said, walking backwards, his strong pace not faltering as his boot buckled over a clod. 'See ye at lunch, then,' he shouted.

'Aye,' Harold called, already plodding back up through the bracken, Matty weaving out in front.

*

A week later, stick in hand, after a heavy night of rain, he was out to check the fells again. The wind was low and the morning clouds gathered in rounded layers, darkening as they moved, gathering weight. He'd checked the gullies on his side of Ard and Knott a few days before, clearing a couple of loose boulders, and he'd built a low shelter with branches and rocks under the old juniper where the winds streaked.

'Good stick this'n,' he agreed as he climbed. 'Best friend next till a dog and that's telling. "Staff," that's it.' The tops were still soggy in parts. He checked the mire areas. There was one to corner off again. His stick didn't sink in deep, but it was water-logged enough for no risks taken. Further on, he found that a top section of Knott had fallen clean off, leaving long slices of grey flint, a sharp-peeled edge leaning over the valley to Wandope; remarkable how it must have come off overnight. He checked underneath. The soil and slate scree hadn't blocked the beck down below which raced, white frothed into itself from the rain. No obvious layers of mud or shingles for the sheep to sink into on the fell side. It would have to be needled, of course, to make sure. Back and forth, to check for mud-slicks.

'Staff'll do it,' he muttered. 'The mud will have fallen somewhere.'

He set to, crooked hand beneath the strong one, counting the digs, so that the pain in his hands was masked with the number, which soon became 'and one, and one'. His back ached so loudly it almost sounded line by line. He hadn't checked through a fellside like this since he was with his dad when a heavy rain season brought the tops of Wandope into the beck and backed it up.

'Ready to shed her coat again and that's it.' He smiled, hearing his father chant 'Clean skin, shiny as a chestnut!'

'Aye,' he said.

The fell was solid enough, a few ledges of scree to be dislodged, but nothing unusual. It was mild considering what had fallen, not much at all, and it felt good to be in the tight valley between Knott and Wandope. He stopped and leant for a moment. The shade of day rested between mountains with the sound of Sail Beck cleansing. 'Fells'd be joined if it weren't for the beck,' he said. 'Brothers.' And once he'd finished, he cooled his sore hands, skin splitting easily to bleed from any pressure these days, and then bent over the fresh speed of water to splash his neck before lying back, damp between the fells, eyes closed, grass and soil muffling any sound.

A while later he decided to check if the newly exposed rock on top was stable. Its cracked slices yet to be mossed, a purple sheen to the glaze. He gave time for the weight of his head to adjust to sitting, then, counting through the strain, he stood and climbed up, zigzagging the steep section at the top, blowing into the wind, which seemed to help. He would hate to be on his tractor now, he thought, seat springing. And when he reached the ridge, he sat on the gentle curve tufted with sedge and waited.

'Nothing like her, nothing like the valley for comfort,' he said, as if talking to the fell. 'Well now, let's have a look, then,' he called, twisting up towards the new rock. And he followed in its direction, a ring ouzel sounding its three sharp calls as he walked further, Great Gable like a bell in the distance, until he was on the steep decline at the end of Knott Rigg. The sky open in front of him with backlit clouds funnelling past Robinson and down to the lake. Then, deep breath, he looked at his feet, *what am I doing here?* The rock had no clues for a moment, then, 'must have missed it,' he said, grabbing his stick with more strength against his now blistered hand and turned back to follow the ridge again towards Sail, rain streaking parts of the sky over Keswick.

He walked on for a while and thought, *can't be further on than this.* But when he looked into the valley, the fellside he'd needled was far behind him again. He'd passed it a second time, and he turned back, a soreness settling in his bones. But when he returned to the place he had needled, there was no bare rock, no purple sheen, no slate leaning over the valley, sleek in newness ... just old, rumbling ground, well trodden by winter, waiting for spring.

He sat again on the verge, looking down across the fell side.

'I did just needle that, didn't I?' he whispered, remembering the slice of slate, long and cracked with its purple hue. 'Wrong colour for here, you bugger,' he whispered. 'It's Wandope has that colour slate. It's a brown here. Was never there, lad, never there.' He looked across the valley to the towering peak of Wandope, purple-grey scree tumbling down its slopes. 'Never there,' his voice now breaking.

Dusk passed unnoticed and evening was only felt like the increase of a vigil towards the valley as he sat, unable to leave, the paths and fells beyond becoming unfamiliar, ring ouzel repeating its call. He wasn't sure what it was when a voice rang behind him and he was shocked, cowering for protection from the hand on his shoulder, until the face stopped peering down and settled close beside him on the verge. The person was talking, he was sure of that, but he strained to keep his sights in the valley, the curve of the banks calming him, and it took a while for the words to pull him away.

'Your hands are blue with cold, Dad. Come on home now and we'll get warmed up, eh?' He looked at his hands. They were stiff. 'Dad?' the voice said. 'Come on, then. Mam'll be worried. Let's go home now, shall we?'

He looked over and saw someone. He might have seen him in a chair or by a coal fire, and yes, a red threaded carpet by the hearth, and oh, the feeling of that cushion in his back and his arms opened to the valley, lifting, held high as he wept in surrender.

'I can't go home,' he sobbed, sweeping his clawed hands to his face, shocked when he was hit with ice. 'Don't look at me.'

'Of course you can,' came from the valley.

'I don't know where I am, lad, a hard truth but.'

'Come on, Dad. It's the same as always. I'll walk with you.'

'You'll walk with me?' he said, catching his breath.

'Of course. We'll walk down together.'

Harold wasn't sure if it was safe. If it was true. The decision twisted in him and he searched for the valley.

'Come on then,' the person said, taking his arm.

He glanced suspiciously to his side.

'Dad, come on. You've never been this long. I'm getting cold. Let's be on,' Stephen said, getting up.

'Here?'

'Yes, Dad. Now we must get down. It's cold,' he said, firmly supporting Harold's arm as he obediently rose, stiff kneed, bent over at first.

'Aye now,' he mumbled, 'let me get my stride,' he said pulling his back painfully straight, realising he was going to walk down the fell. 'Thank you,' he choked, looking over to the person, aware now that his lips were numb, blotting his speech. 'Thank you,' he spat to the valley, the cradle that watched like an old lady, the lifeblood of water sounding even in shadow. And they began, arm held tight, to descend in a stagger.

He awoke to soft, white cotton and the smell of washed blankets, a moment folded in before the pain. Heat rose from his guts and burned his skin. He went to fling the covers off the bed and found his hands were cramped and blistered, peeling like bark. He pushed the weight of blankets off with his arm and swung his legs around to sit. His head waved as if it were filled with water, a bruised feeling dangling like a pendulum. He was consumed by it. He took a deep breath, the pendulum beginning to settle, and he squinted around the room. Green curtains closed around the bed, seamed with daylight. He went towards them for some air and was hit by an electric shock, bright yellow, throwing him to the floor. It hovered over him as his nerves convulsed, the ground shuddering in hurried thuds till the room darkened and sharp wire pricked his skin.

Someone lifted his back and helped him to the feeling of a bed, which he could no longer see, and pushed something sharp into his arm, shocking his skin again. When he woke up the room was dark with heavy, green-velvet curtains closed over a window. Daylight was shining through the gaps, but he couldn't tell the time. *Should be up and out by now.*

The next time he woke it was to polished white cotton, folded and pulled tight over his legs like an envelope. Esther's head was buried in her arms at his side. He reached out to touch her dark curls. They were like silk in his sore hand and she looked up.

'So sorry, love,' he said and she smiled, saying something he couldn't hear. When he looked around, straight walls flanked him. They kept him still. Greyhound in wait. And the fluorescent light was fiercer than midday sun opening the back of his eyes.

'Keep your eyes shut,' he said, metal clanging in the distance.

'Hello Dad,' someone said, and the covers moved around him.

'Ower hot,' Harold mumbled. 'Must be Stephen, that you?' he said, straining to see.

'Mam'll be back in a minute. Let's get these straightened.'

Harold flinched at the touch. 'No.'

'Just fold them back neatly then and keep the sheet, eh?'

Harold ruffled his feet and reluctantly accepted the feeling of weight on his shins. His skin itched.

'Brought you these.'

'What, lad?'

'These.'

And Harold flinched at the blur moving up to him,

touching his nose and ears. He pushed it away and then sat, slowly noticing the room had become brown; evening-valley brown and his eyes rested. 'Oh,' he said.

'Better?'

'Aye, better.'

'You've got sunglasses on, Dad. We won't mention the Duran Duran pattern on them. We'll just let that one go by!'

'Duram duram?' he asked.

'Aye, they're from the rugby raffle. You know, Duran Duran. The "dance band", you call it.'

'Oh.'

'Got them at the end of season last year.'

'Very good,' he smiled and moved his head to free the strain in his neck.

'You look like Stevie Wonder now, Dad!' Stephen laughed, Harold joining in.

A few weeks later Harold obediently waited, hunched on the edge of the hospital bed. His skin was scrubbed under his best grey jacket, polished town-shoes squeezing his feet. Bags packed, they walked down the tall hallway, Esther moving him this way and that, a swish or creak to the lino. The car door was opened for him and he sat listless as she buckled him in. Back at the farm, she fluffed a cushion on his chair by the fire. A different chair maybe, bigger than it was, his elbows reaching out to rest.

X

Spring 1994

Esther

Friday and the stone kitchen was dark. The electricity would be off till Clive fixed the fuse box. Esther stood to write the familiar Friday list, used to ignoring the burning in her hips. She wouldn't be out long, not wanting to leave Harold, his skin now like new wax; days emptying him to a shadow. *He's almost brittle*, she thought. *Maybe even a bitterness in him sometimes, though he thinks it's secret.* She needed to visit her mother and talk to the nurses about him staying there. Depression and dementia were unpredictable and the doctors talked about him going back to the hospital, which drained her and silenced him. She was lost in those grey corridors, and the sounds from other patients seemed infectious.

The stone top was cool, in fact the kitchen was peaceful without light. It made her stop. She tied a ribbon around a tin, as she always did for her mother. Lemon drizzle cake this week. She would protect Harold as much as she could, she thought, her resolve immediately weakened by the truth that she might have to stand by him, empty armed, as it happened again. The idea made her feel weak.

Out in the yard Harold was sweeping. It had hardly been a week since he was home, but his presence was familiar, savoured, watched; huddled as he walked, sheep pushed not hushed, trailed not gathered. Naps in the day, like her mother did for years. Still there, deep down. Memories to be enjoyed when he settled enough to talk again, vulnerable in his silence. *We'll make the most of him. Just needs a routine.*

She walked back down the corridor with her grandmother's limp and sorted the list. Her father had the same every week. She went through a phase of going to local farms for vegetables, catching up on news, but for a few years now, since her mother went into St Anne's, she preferred to spend the time there and shopped on the high street.

She laid a cold lunch out on the table, plates overturned on top to protect the meat, tomatoes and coleslaw. Dishcloth on the bread, a familiar smell of fresh yeast, another tin of lemon cake to the side. Stephen was on the fells, Clive was in the yard with Harold, clearing out the barn and Catherine was still upstairs, *best not to waken her if she is resting.*

As she drove she felt heavy in the seat and thought of old times to talk about with Harold. Becoming a father, becoming more like his own father George as Stephen grew up with songs and stories around the house. And Stephen would have stories about times on the fells. She rested in the memories of Harold as a new father for a while and saw them so vividly, she worried a sheep or deer would walk out in front of the car; kept leaning forward, blinking to look at the road. When she arrived at Cockermouth she went to the wool shop on her way to St Anne's. *Blue and purple this week, though Mam's often not used the last lot.* When she got to the home, the nurses were full of chat as usual, bells going off from the residents' rooms, the smell of lunch being made in the kitchens. They seemed pleased with the idea of having Harold, but couldn't say if it was possible and made a time for her to come again with his local doctor to talk things through. As usual, her mother wasn't in the sitting room with the others, watching TV. She was sitting on the chair by her bed, eyes to the window, magazine on her lap, a scrumble of part-knitted wool on the bed.

'Hello, Mam,' she said, slightly high-voice.

'Oh, hello Esther, that's good now.'

'Clouds and rain again today. Not too bad.' Esther hummed, pleased to be recognised.

'Oh, is it?'

'Aye, and I've brought you some more colours for the blanket.'

'The blanket?'

'Aye, the blanket you're making – look, there it is.' And she lifted the square sections of red, blue and green.

'Oh,' her mother said, reaching out to them as if they were work to be done and setting them on her knee, quickly absorbed in making the wools hang in the same direction.

'I got you a blue and a purple. Lovely shade of blue, look.' She held it out, reading the label. 'Azure, they call it. And Purple Mist.' Her mother looked up. Esther laughed. 'I know, Purple Mist! How do you decide to call it that?' Her mother rolled her eyes and got back to work, soon putting her hand out for the wool. Esther sat to the sound of needles clipping, looking at the car park, warm air around them with the sweet smell of ointments. 'Good Friday today, Mam,' she said, still looking out. 'Easter Sunday soon.'

Her mother looked up. 'Is Mam coming?'

'Oh, well, I expect so,' Esther said, probably entering into being her sister for a moment.

'Right then.'

'What'll we be doing?' she asked, wondering what she would say.

'Oh, it'll be church as usual, I expect.'

'What will Grandma's family be doing?'

'Grandma? Esther, you mean?'

'Yes.' Esther enjoyed the same name as her grandmother for a moment.

'Oh,' she said and closed her eyes tight. 'That was a shame.'

'What was?'

'Should have done it.'

'Done what, Mam?'

'The sheet of course, you know,' she said with a side glance as if Esther had been tricking her.

'Yes,' Esther tried to join in.

'And burned it.'

'Burned it? Why would she burn it?'

'Not her, us.'

'How would we do that then? I can't remember.' Esther asked gently. Too many questions could disturb her; even the past was now hard to grasp sometimes.

161

'Do you mean putting the strip from an old rag out on Saturday, Mam? She didn't do that, did she?'

'Oh, she liked all that.'

'When did she?'

'When we were young. Did it all. Is there any tea going?'

'I would like to know, Mam. Is that what it was, cotton in the porch?' Esther realised she was now herself again with her mother, and hoped that the bridge between now and her memories would hold.

'No, come on with the tea and biscuits.'

'Do the sheet . . .' Esther said, hoping her mother would finish the thought.

'The last sheet. Did it for her mam. Always would have. Taken from her bed and kept till the Saturday. Some bury it in a box in wait for the day but it's not in the rules that you have to.' She continued adjusting the squares so they were in a straight line. 'Then hung out for Holy Week.'

'Hung where?'

'Ripped not cut. Now, where's the tea?'

'And then burned?'

'Of course, Sunday dawn,' she added in a curt tone.

Esther was confused. She remembered people being laid out on their final sheet for visitors through the night before the burial but she didn't remember her grandmother saying anything else, even in secret. She thought of the imprint of Christ on linen that was kept somewhere. 'Is it called a shroud?'

'Sheet,' her mother tutted. 'And tied with three knots on both ends,' she called to the window as if someone was there. 'Father, Son and Holy Spirit. Ripped, never cut.'

Esther waited to see if she would say any more.

'Why didn't we do it?' she said under her breath.

'No,' her mother straightened the squares again and picked up her needles. 'Not those things at the Manor. Mind, it wasn't right to.' She stopped and scolded herself, looking over with fleeting desperation. 'We just washed it,' she coughed, her voice tailing away.

They sat for a while, her mother knitting slowly, looking unusually vulnerable even childlike and then her mother suddenly said, a little choked, 'But with the right hymn, mind. She didn't like those modern ones.'

'No she didn't,' Esther said, tearful herself to see her mother like that. 'Is there one specially for it?'

'"I Know a Fount",' she snapped.

Esther stayed another half hour, remembering her grandmother, wondering what she was like when she was young. How religious. *We were three generations caught between worlds at the Manor. All the changes she'd seen must have made life so unfamiliar.* She was glad of the routine they'd had. *Kept us home,* she thought.

After her visit she walked down the street slower than usual and, once in the shop, the aisles seemed to clear her mind with the ease of choosing and measuring out vegetables. At the till there was another poster for the Easter Parade. 'Hoping for good weather,' she said to Dianne, who worked there a few days a week while her children were at school.

'Oh aye, the bonnets'll dye everything if we've rain. They've been using felt tips on crêpe paper at school, drawing all sorts.'

'Best put them in an Easter smock and wellies, then!'

'That'll be right,' she said. 'Good name for an old shirt. Draw a bunny on it, eh?' They laughed.

On her way back from shopping, after stacking her father's kitchen shelves and leaving a note about the vigil that night and Sunday, Esther decided to stop at the church. She liked it when there was no one there. The shape of it, the inside, the windows. It taught her as much by the way it stood as anything else. As she was going in, she saw a flicker of someone around the side and darted into the porch, unnerved. *No reason others shouldn't be here*, she said to herself, surprised at the fright. A scuff and she turned to see him, thin shoulders and wide white-blue eyes watching. His pupils were as small as grains of sand. And then he slowly smiled, hungrily, holding his stare, leaning his face forward, straining a long veined neck. She felt trapped. A gradual step back gave her the space to reach for the door, his eyes darting between the movement of her arm and their locked stare. As she pulled, the door creaked. The noise made him flinch like a hound, startled, hunched, smirking as if he relished the game. She bolted in not knowing if she would feel him on her back. The bang resounded like a cannon inside the church, shunting the lock across with a slac to the sound of him scratching on the other side. The strangeness panicked her and she rushed, echoing steps, to the vestry for another way out, but the door to it was locked. All doors in the church were now locked. Sweat pushed through her. She would have to wait. He was dirty, muddy and worn. *Must be sleeping rough. Wait.* A horror came over her. *Was that Isaac, Jim's grandson?* It didn't make sense that he would look at her like that. *Could it be him?* Then the church went dark. *Clouds,* she thought, and wondered if she should go back to the door. *Was he really that bad?* And then came the sound of scrambling, silence, then a scuffling further around. She followed the sound appearing and disappearing along the side wall to the back and then stood by the altar listening to scraping and tapping. Not prepared for the shock of his shadow lifting into the window, hunched at first, arms reaching flat against the glass, pulling himself up to stand, his legs turned out to fit on the ledge, arms stretched to the stone sides. She cowered at the sight, staggering back. The man towered above Mary and Martha, boned and cross-like, lined with lead. Head flickering through Christ like a bird; small eye, flinching to see in.

The church echoed with her steps as she ran, slipping down the aisle, slithering the lock out. She stopped for a moment. Should she leave? He must need help. Even her body was confused. She edged part way around the side but there was no sign of him. So, darting down the steps to her car, key funnelling for the ignition, she drove to call for help as if she were an arrow with a target.

When she got home ready to call, she found the doctor had visited without warning and given Harold some new medicine. Catherine said it was to help him rest. Esther had no patience; frustrated the doctor had visited without her there, without her questions. She called the vicarage and then the

Bridge Hotel. 'It might have been Isaac, but if it was, he wasn't himself.' She felt embarrassed in the telling. All he'd done was climb onto the window.

'Most likely will be,' said Mr Sadler from the hotel. 'He's been lost a few times.'

'He would have known the church though.'

'Aye, but he forgets. Not been right with the anxiety and then the asthma. He gets what they call episodes.'

'I didn't know.'

'Well, the family's quiet about it, likely.'

'I wasn't sure he recognised me.'

'Always was a sensitive lad, but lately it's become a problem. Been in Garlands for a while. It's a worry.'

'Poor lad, I didn't know he'd been in hospital. I'll call Jim.'

'No bother, I'll call him and we'll get it sorted. He'll be grateful for the news.'

'Send him my best and anything he needs.'

'Will that.'

In defeat, she took herself upstairs, needing space. Harold lay, arm hanging over the side, breath deep in his chest. At night he was sensitive to any movement, crooked hand tucked close to his chest, waking and turning, dry cracked skin blotting the sheets, and now she could carefully lift his arm over the blankets and sit on the side of the bed, watching, his hand in hers, his wrist, ruddy-pink skin with fine brown hairs, and he didn't wake. *It will do him good to finally sleep*, she thought, worried he was so flattened by it.

She'd wanted to light a candle for her mother and grandmother in the church. *Oh, that was strange*, she shuddered.

Wonder where he is now. She climbed onto the bed, Harold's hand still held. Her thoughts so full she was close to weeping, and she curled into Harold's sleeping back, his woolly jumper moving with his breath, soon lulled into the brink of sleep herself, as if the two of them were sheltered in a small alcove. It was the first time she'd been able to hold him since he was back from hospital. In fact, it had been years since he could sleep with them resting on each other. But, her fall into sleep was far away. As were the days before Harold was ill. And the image of a twitching man peering above the altar seemed etched into her. She breathed out, trying to let it go and her grandmother came to mind. *Everything feels so slippery. Just hold onto it and it's gone.* Her grandmother's life and her ways with it. Not honoured the way she would have liked. Disgrace at the Manor. She thought of doing the sheet for the dead herself and flushed with embarrassment. 'I'm no better than the rest,' she whispered. 'Frightened of mockery.' But the worst that could happen is that it would make Stephen laugh, if he noticed, he was so busy now. She should have taken a hymn book from the church. 'I Know a Fount,' she whispered.

Harold slept through the day and into the following evening. When Esther went to bed she lay on her side, hand resting on his shoulder again. His sweat was bitter in the sheets and a guttural snore kept her awake. She rubbed his back gently, pressing hope into him with her palms. His weight comforted her, like oak.

XI

Spring 1994

Harold

'I'm not settling in bed, Trin, I'll be out on t'farm today,' Harold said watching Catherine sweep the blankets with her buckled fingers to smooth any wrinkles.

'No, lad,' she said, tottering around the chest of drawers. 'You're home to rest and I'll bring you a cup of tea.'

'Aye, but not in here, not daytime here,' he said, straining to sit up.

Catherine turned her head to the side, as if to hear properly. He waited and she said, 'You're right, lad. We'll make do somehow. Let's open the window for now and have a think.'

'Right,' he said, frustrated with his regular need to bolt.

'Well then, that's better, I'll get us some tea.'

'Right.'

He listened to her slow creak down the stairs, swung his legs over to stand, shocked by the sharp pain, catching his breath, and followed the sounds below. The hall was lantern low in its glow and sucked him out to the yard. Like a moth to light. And at last he breathed the spread of fells in front, felt them give space to his mind. Nothing between him and them. Robinson ever gratified in front, Knott Rigg, Ard and Sail gladly leaning in from behind, filling the yard with their scent, opening him, fizzing his body with ... lifting him with ... spreading him onto their tops, into the sky, the air brightening him with ... all he could hear himself think was that it was with glory, yes, a glorious day.

And it was Catherine's small hands that pulled him back from the gate, unable as he was to see or hear her. Sound still absorbed in the bright. But it was her fingers clasping his hand that led him, as blind as an old shire horse, back to the porch and his chair by the fire without his paper, objects outlined in blue. Soon being given a cup of hot sweet tea, too sweet, he thought, drinking it and seeing her, Catherine, on the other chair. Hardly there, like someone remembered.

'Where is everyone?' he asked.

'Market,' she said, wearily.

'Not having tea, Trin?'

'Oh I didn't think. Well, I'll have one later.'

And then he was sitting on the edge of the bed again, watching the softness of his brown slippers brush against each other, thoughts circling in the back of his mind like a bird, a damp taste of fells in the night. He'd slept, he knew that. Must have dreamt he walked outside. The pills Dr Brown had given were good ones. He still felt the sleep on his breath, even though he was sitting up. He looked around and saw the dresser. Framed black and white photographs and a china vase with painted flowers. It was Catherine's room. Had he slept there? He slapped his thigh, 'Get on with it,' and stood for a while holding his breath. Then he walked, heavy-footed, to his room, a little burning in his stomach, unnerved by how quiet it was downstairs. It was a relief to be in his own bedroom, reaching for his clothes, wondering what was happening with the farm. When he got to the sitting room it was empty and the clock chimed quarter to. Catherine was in the kitchen. She didn't notice him at first and he wondered why he stood quietly at the door, watching her. It made her seem vulnerable.

'Oh, hello, lad. You've had a good sleep. Would you like something to eat?'

He wasn't sure if he was hungry.

'Cup of tea?'

He nodded. 'Where is everyone?'

'Well, Joe and Stephen are working on something, I don't know what. And Esther's out.'

'Oh,' he said, trying to remember what jobs were on today. He looked back at Catherine.

'Don't worry, lad, it'll all come to you,' she said, walking to the larder.

He woke again and asked if it was morning, waiting for a reply. It was his room. His back was shaking and he tried to swallow, but it stuck in his throat. *Must have a virus again*, he thought, *just sleep it off. Ah, there she is*, her soft, pale arm over the covers next to him. His Esther. He reached out and felt his rough hand on her skin. *Can't lose her*.

He could focus now, a regular time given to be in the sitting room. It was marked by the pendulum clock, whose click he hummed in his mind throughout the hour, before he returned upstairs. The obedience made him feel thin. A little more each day. The following week he was up for three hours and exhausted by it. Still endurance, still waiting, always wanting to rinse his face with wild cool water. Catherine bringing him sweet tea.

Another week and Harold was on new medication again. It made a metallic taste in his mouth. And more drowsy, like a hangover, but he was suddenly able to feel the shape of a room. Lean on the back of his chair and greet people, and soon he could go for a walk, as long as it wasn't too far. The evening coals no longer mulled his thoughts, but he was able to hum a tune to block the clock if its rhythm came into his head too much, and walk the hall when he got cramps. He tried to bring the feeling of the fells home with him, let them wash into him, like they used to. They were with him in the sitting room for moments, maybe, or was it memories of them? The objects in the room took his attention, one by one. A surprise to see the next. And he spent a lot of his time trying to temper his annoyance with details, the edges and alignment of things. An intrusion of unexpected demands, or mess, or sound could take over him. Like the way Stephen shovelled coal onto the fire, grating the stone under the iron basket, Harold's body tightening with every shunt. He could see the tension on the back of his son's neck. Knowing his father was annoyed, but never speaking of it. 'That bloody clock,' Harold would say.

And he'd get irritated with the tea, how long it took and if the plates clipped, especially when his hands shook, flinching. Esther sitting opposite him with questions. The soft smile on her face which used to draw him into himself, let his skin spread for the evening, now landed on him like tin.

As time wore on and evenings folded onto one another, he closed. Tight tired, pushing into his bones to keep strong, digging in and secretly becoming disgusted with the man he was. The madness in his head, because that was what he saw, madness and nothing more.

He relinquished hours up for early nights in grief and waited for the ache to go, sometimes for hours, lying wooden on his side, not wanting Esther to see who he was. Eyes held shut, so still that he might avoid the feeling of sand underneath his lids. When she came, arm reaching around him, he controlled his inbreath through his throat, like a straw. Not cupping her hand to him. Knowing that if he touched her she would feel the darkness in him and it would hurt her.

A smooth stone, rounded, with a slight grain to the touch, was in his dream one night. Grey and worn by the sea, with the hiss of cool waves pulling. And someone holding it in their hand. A man. Taken into his pocket on a journey and now given back. His hand stretched through the waves, the sound resting his breath, deepening. He reached towards Harold, tide seeping forward and drawing him back to spread across the sea. Wide. It felt like someone close, not his father, though. Flat cap, shirtsleeves rolled up. And then the man walked on the beach and took the stone out of his pocket to show him.

He woke to a sense of calm, waiting a long time till everyone was up, before he could search for John's photo. See his hands, if it was him in the dream. He shifted piles on the

172

tops of shelves inside Catherine's wardrobe. Then he found the suitcase under her bed and dug through a shawl, pewter cup, soft brown leather purse, china box and pipe, tumbling them out to the sides, and found the old bundles of letters, pleated flat like greaseproof paper. He pulled a thin ribbon, his crooked hand frustrated at the knot, crumpling pages to part them, almost see-through, lifting a small clump by mistake and read:

However rewarding God's work is, at nights I find it hard to leave the trenches, especially our Fred, Wilson and Jack. I visit the memorial I built on the nearest peak and though alone, I take regular services there asking for absolution. Unsure if His mercy ought to be given. And if such a gift is bestowed, how one might begin to live with it ...

He sat back for a moment. *High peaks they would be*, he thought. And looking at the papers he saw a wedge, longer than the rest with a black ink drawing just showing. He pulled it, expecting a picture, and as the top letters loosened, some spilled onto the floor with a slap, others drifting. It was a drawing of a Chinaman with a long plait.

Drawing by Mrs Murray.
Report from Longtan Medical Centre.
For Parish readings.

He pulled back a couple of pages, smudging the old ink, leaning over and read:

173

A young man came to the hospital with a broken leg. His family then arrived to collect him and it turned out they wanted him back because they …

He lifted the top of that bunch and slapped it to his side on the bed, digging in to find John. The new letter began:

Dear Catherine,

May God be with you. You will be pleased to hear I have now set up a Dispensary in Yichang on the 3 important market days held every month …

He turned the bundle over, focusing in, seeing something in the back of his mind and leant over the suitcase, divining for another bundle. These were worn. He leant over one like a map, sweat blotting the paper, feeling the dents of his grandmother's hands.

… your news has now reached the monastery and arrangements have been made for a descent in two days to an area where I will be able to place a phone call to you. It will be four days in total before I am able to call, taking consideration of two days for the descent from St Catherine's. I have a few letters here for you, which have not yet been sent. I enclose them for reading at another time. During the next two days the monks have allowed me to sit vigil with them on Mount Sinai, for which I am grateful. We will be on the side of the

mountain through the night. As the peaks join across the continents, I will join with you in prayer.

As with birth, death is rarely easy and I hope that Mother was not ill for long and had a peaceful end. She will have followed to the other side with tenacity, of that I am sure.

'For thou art with me, thy rod and thy staff they comfort me.'

Forgive my leaning on scripture at this time. I am mindful that simple words may be more helpful, though better in the quiet speaking of them at chosen moments around ordinary days than in the writing of them. Forgive, therefore my hurried writing. I see how hope so easily becomes a plea and, as with the Psalms, I find I plead for home. Mother said that in grief Our Lady Mary lends us her arms. Wise arms that knew the deepest despair, lifting her son off the Cross and carrying him to the tomb. I pray for Her strength and companionship. To thank Mother for our home would never be enough. They say we enter grace at the Eucharist, open mouthed. But to see grace is rare. Most of us must be content with the faith that it can be found. Our Lady Mary saw it. Mother gave it.

And so, dear Catherine I wait for two days in this land of pilgrimage, as, in truth, is all land. Though this land remembers it most keenly. In these night vigils, some of the monks are said to have visions of Christ at dawn. I have never had one myself, but will be content to feel the power of full-hearted waiting. May

the veil of heaven be drawn back and His eternal light
be a balm to our souls.

> *Come, Holy Ghost, our hearts inspire,*
> *let us Thine influence prove;*
> *source of the old prophetic fire,*
> *fountain of life and love.*

I pray our voices join upon the singing.

'Aye, we would sing that hymn on the fells,' Harold said with a feverish memory of his father and grandfather belting out the words one evening on Haystacks. He scrambled into the suitcase for a hymn book and pulled up what was an old bible. Surprised to see letters folded into it, he tore one open and read:

Dear George,

'Father,' Harold cried turning the page as if he would see a photo.

... said that God's love must be as cleansing as ...

The tear went across and a section below was outlined in pencil:

Confusion strikes any man in this war. There is no shame in it. You ask for my solution and I give you no reason or plot. Anxiety appears as a building around us, fortressed from the land. The only remedy I know is a bid for freedom. And, my lad, when the boots in your hallway are not to hand and the fells miles away, the bid is to be made in the mind and heart. Take yourself home, lad. Fill your imagination. Remember the walk above the farm, the sound of morning, the bracken crisp in spring and the bleating sheep as you arrive. In a foreign night, adjust your eyes to the half-moon over Crummock Water. To be sure, unwelcome sounds and movements trick us all from our thoughts. But they are never defeated by confrontation, only escape. Return home again and again as if the place were in your very breath. And if, my lad, you are anything like me and have worries to confess, imagine the peak of Sail, Red Pike or some other fell and climb it to reconcile with your maker. I find the old words of confession help me speak and renew the faith that I am heard by God, even when, as is often the case, I know it not. Tradition: a cornerstone stronger than any confusion or anxiety. You will find your own version, George, but look for it in the twin peaks of land and tradition. A tabernacle of grace between them.

The words settled in him, thin paper spread over the bed and on the floor, parting towards the fells. *Aye*, he thought, a heavy pressure to his head. *It's there, or nothing.* 'Old ways, my lad, old ways. Fells are fair-handed.' *They're fair. Have to remember that.* He'd fallen into darkness. Skyless black. It stuck like tar. He'd lost his family and he'd lost the truth. Bound by defeat like a prisoner. But the fells were where he belonged. They made him who he was. His heart burst for Esther and the lad. 'If the mountains can't clean my bones, blow the dirt out of me, then nothing will,' he said. 'And they'd be better without me, the poison in me.' He couldn't let it near them, let it taint them. He had to protect them. Cleanse. Yes, he'd make a bid for it, his belly full of conviction. He would pull on his boots and go.

XII

Spring 1994

Esther

The kitchen was dark, clouds hovering. It didn't feel right to have the light on. For this, Esther wanted to be alone. She waited a moment, poised, a firm grip in hand, elbows out, thinking of her grandmother, old white sheet taken from her bed that morning, spread in folds on the floor. And then she leant in, broad hands, back pressing forward, pulling. She needed to stop, unpick the hem and tease the edge before she could begin the tear, before it creaked and then ripped shrill in the kitchen, her arms reaching out as the cotton moaned and frayed into long, thin strips. And as she tore, fists clenched, pulling her chest, she saw her grandmother laid out in her best dress, the oak coffin hard on their dining table, family sitting on chairs, squashed together through the night. And then she was with her grandmother on one of their walks, looking for flowers in a light rain. She ripped and saw her mother making the evening meal, vibrant in her plans for more work, and now by the window in St Anne's. She ripped and began to weep, leaning into the tear, arms pulling tight, her cry mixed with the sound, the rent, and soon she heard herself wail, fluff rising in low light.

And then, flushed wet cheeks, she sat, still, out of breath, looking down at the frayed pile on the floor, white streaking the tiles. Light-headed, curious. Her back slowly wakening to an ache, hands wrung out.

As she limped up towards the garden, strip of sheet in hand, she remembered her grandmother's pace slowing in the fells, ending as a heel-drawn shuffle between rooms. Once she'd looped the frayed cotton over the oak branch and tied three knots on either side, she stood back. 'Hope you've found peace,' she said. 'You are still loved.' And as she watched the clean sheet exposed to the night, she realised that Catherine's strips were more worn every year. *Must be the same ones, never burned*, she thought. It showed something uncomfortably private about her.

That evening Harold didn't come home for his supper. He hadn't been with Stephen all day. After the meal Stephen headed out to find him. He wouldn't be too far away. Before the hospital there were places he would stay into the night. Often the same ones. Once he was the other side of Catbells by Derwent Water, but usually he was nearby. He'd not stayed out like that for a while. Maybe it was a good sign, she thought, and then hung her head. Maybe it wasn't, but it was no good taking the fells away from him. She watched the silent weariness in Stephen as he set off.

'Come back for help if you need it,' she called to a nod as he left. These last few months had taken the conversation out of him. Out of her, too. As if they were on the edge of a large wave, trying to live a normal day.

She cleared the table and went into the kitchen to get Catherine's tray ready. She'd forgotten to ask Stephen if he'd seen the strip of sheet dangling in the garden. It would be there the next morning, if it hadn't blown away. It would be wet by now. *They can eat as soon as they're home*, she thought, putting lamb in the stove to warm for a late supper, and went upstairs, tray in hand.

Night set through open grey into wine-black and still no news. She hovered by the phone, wondering if she should call Clive or the neighbours to help look for Harold and, having done that, she seemed to panic more. After a while Stephen came home to say he was off again and a group had gathered to go through the fells with an ordered plan, so they would know where they'd searched. People were kind to be out looking again.

She sat, focusing on the fells as if her thoughts might touch him. The rest of the sheet needed to be cut into neat rags for cleaning, but one look and it felt wrong to use it like that. She left the door open, bread and cheese on the table, and walked out. A line stretched across the moon as she entered the garden, basket in hand. It was almost yellow, but shone pale white onto the grass. The strip of sheet she'd tied was stuck around the oak branch and, rather than hang up the other strips, something made her prise open the knots and as soon as the strip was unwound she was out of the garden and up the path, resting her basket on a boulder at the foot of the fell for a moment, a stony dart moth lifting from its sleep. And then, in a straight line she climbed up the high slope, almost pulled, leaning into her steps. When she reached the old juniper, dark trunk bent in the night, she set to, tying each piece to the three branches so that the sheets hung like a tabernacle, catching the rain. Their white bowed under the dark clouds as sky beneath sky, stains of rust from the occasional branch. She wondered where Harold was, feeling she was somehow near him. And that her steps were like her grandmother's, even her great-grandmother's; stopping every now and then to sing or read the hymn, humming the chorus, a strain of grief as she tied.

> 'I know a fount where sins are washed away
> I know a place where night is turned to day
> Burdens are lifted, blind eyes made to see'

The branches were tied, so she tore smaller strips and knotted what was left to tall grasses and bracken, slowly laying it out, frayed onto the land, bending and swaying in the wind, hanging over the tops, knotting three times, as she had been told, her fingers pricked from thorns and wet from passing rain. Stooping. And the clouds opened, lifting the white, deepening the dark, while she leant in, again and again somehow with the rhythm of washing day, the tying, the hanging.

> 'Expand thy wings, celestial Dove,
> brood o'er our nature's night;
> on our disordered spirits move,
> and let there now be light.'

Markers, she thought. *Flags dreamt on.* Her and Harold's sleep given to the fell, to the wind. Their warmth spread like seeds. All will be well.

> 'God, through the Spirit we shall know
> if thou within us shine,
> and sound, with all thy saints below,
> the depths of love divine.'

And as she walked back down, limping to protect her knees, she looked back to find the tree cupped sleep to the sky over a sweep of white knots and trailed cotton. *Lazarus*, she thought. *Lazarus laid out on the fell. Hope in night. Wounds healed. Promise.*

XIII

Spring 1994

Stephen

Stephen found him. Hard-curled in sheepskin around the roots of the tree. He was in Mellbreak valley on the far side of Crummock Water. Pale, cold and matted into a fleece. Rocks piled against his feet from the current. Slumped against the bark of a tall juniper.

He sat with him, peeled rattles of knotted bark against Harold's cheek. Hardened weeping. When he went to put his jacket over him, cover his naked chest and his head, he bent forward lifting Harold's back, bones hard as wood now, so he could dig in behind, gathering him in, rocking slightly, respected. Streams whittled around them through heavy grasses and stones to the lake, ringing as they dropped through tunnels and he found himself whispering so low that the words hardly left his mouth. 'You're all right now, lad. All right now.'

After some time, dawn broke and he looked up to find his father's shirt tied and tangled into the branches and with all his strength he tried to see the valley again; the lake, tops of the fells. Clouds spread gold across Rannerdale and

Robinson. They lit one to another like candles towards Ard. It was painful to look with the weight of his father on him, arms clenched tight, even the outline of it.

Days later, they buried him, Stephen and Joe shoulder to shoulder, arms linked to take the weight of the coffin as they walked with the other bearers. The clouds were thick, bulbous grey but layered; fast moving above and slow, almost still, below. Rain hung in the air, sticking to people's faces like heat as the priest read prayers around the sliced, opened ground. *In my house there are many mansions*. Then people gathered in a line, a silent line, which wove around the graves, moving forward, a step at a time, for a handful of earth to throw down, drumming the coffin. Stephen stood next to the priest at the head of the opening, unable to catch anyone's eye. His mother, Esther, and Catherine behind them, waiting. When the people dispersed Stephen gouged his spade into the heap of soil to fill his father's ground as only a son could. Dig him in, buried, safe, lost. Joe and some others helped once it was half filled; a heavy sweat until the earth was returned as a mound, almost as if Harold had been buried above ground, unstamped; no one able to stamp the land in.

The wake was at the farm, Stephen's new tractor standing still in the yard. Harold's boots in the porch. Black suits and dresses darkening the hall and sitting room, white plates of food in hand. Catherine looked small, leaning to the side as she walked in slow and certain steps to and from the kitchen, back bent over a tray. Esther spent most of the time at the sink, her friends cramming the kitchen like a bucket of coals, tea towels in wait, waking her to questions of where things should be stacked. Halfway through, she left the noise, *like a fire in the house*, she thought, and went up to her old room, the spare room she'd been in when she first arrived, unmarried. She looked towards her garden, the window a barrier, eyes forward, waiting. Some time later Catherine came up and perched beside her on the bed with a sigh whispering 'house should be salted for me'. And they sat together in dark-clothed silence, the cottage rattling.

'You stay here for a rest and I'll go down to Stephen,' Esther said.

'Be down shortly.'

Esther got to the sitting room and Jim was in an armchair, stick to the side. He stumbled to get up at the sight of her, hand shaking to put his plate down, unbalanced in his stride to greet her, arms wide, 'So sorry, lass. Never a better man. Him or his father.' He gripped her shoulders, almost a hug. 'And thank you for helping Isaac, he's not doing well these days,' he said, keeping his gaze. 'We're here for you, lass, any time.' Stephen was in the corner, he looked thin. Her father and a small circle of men were around him with clusters of guests waiting to give their condolences, talking quietly as if they were in line at church. White collars starched around weathered skin. 'It's a rare mould that made the likes of him,' someone said.

Stephen felt himself nod and thank people without listening. Suits wrapped around them like lead. He wanted to open the window and let some air into the room. It seemed full of their breath.

By early afternoon the house was emptied of guests and looked shabby, as if the edges had been worn by the day.

Joe pulled the two comfy chairs back to the fireside, the sound of crockery and borrowed bowls fading. Stephen sat with him, hardly noticing Joe or the sounds. And they rested, chairs brimmed with their tired bodies, Stephen sometimes staring at a lone saucer left to the side of the hearth, wondering what cake the crumbs came from. John's bible on the dresser now with another old bible on top.

'If you want food, the leftovers are in the larder,' came from the hallway. They nodded.

After an hour or so, Stephen found the energy to move, and as he passed, Joe caught his arm. 'Done well, lad,' he said, still looking at the fire. 'Your father and grandfather would be proud.' His grip seemed louder than his words. Stephen passed the kitchen and went out to the porch. Let the wind blow the day out of him. By the time he'd walked down to the gate looking out towards the fells, he knew he had to go back to Mellbreak. To walk there, by the lake, to hang his head by the trees, to confess into the waters and find what his father was looking for.

Esther was in her old room that night. Even the furniture there was too familiar, the curtainless window a black mirror. She turned the light off, eased by what became a haze outside, soon searching the burnt line of peaks in her mind as if Harold hadn't been found. By the early hours, she felt like sitting defeated in the garden, wind buffeting her face in Catherine's chair, sea of dark oak leaves hissing above, when she heard Stephen get ready to leave. The evening before he'd hardly the words to ask if she would mind him walking in the fells for a few days. She knew he would go back to Crummock Water, to the valley. He hadn't taken it in; looked bewildered when he told her where he'd found Harold. But she said nothing about him going back there other than that he should take food. Nor did she ask if Joe was going with him. He needed to unbind the last few days in his own way. Have a clear breath of things with no demands. Though she was worried that there would be memories in the fells and grief wasn't kind. She stayed at the top of the stairs listening to him packing by the door and once he left, she quietly followed to the dark porch and watched his lonely pace facing the silhouette of fells until they took him.

Stephen passes the juniper tree with a quiet tap. The bark is rough to the touch, moonlight showing the layers. His backpack is full. Hemp at his side. His pace is steady, scanning the land in front, sifting through the swollen buds, relieved it is always the same place, seasons changing, bits fallen, rusted, mossed, sunken, but always the same. The wind is low in the grasses. It softens his tread, drawing him on. And the glow behind the clouds lifts and cleanses the land with new water.

A few sheep notice as he climbs Ard, musty air filling them to scrummage. Some follow, weighing his stride, rustling through the heather simmering at their feet, flecks of white spring sewn in. And there he settles on the shoulder, at the edge of the mires. Just over the curve, so the lights of the farm aren't seen.

While it's dark, the sheep are quiet, huddled in a dry gully, away from the cold. Hemp lies to one side, ready to pounce into his bowed tracking, thundering low across the grasses.

Stephen lies on the other, just along from them, dug in, carved under a ledge. As it rains, he pulls his bivi bag on, hearing the tapper sound of water on the hood over his head, settling his thoughts, thick smell of earth in his breath. The smell is so familiar that his father could be standing at the gate looking out.

He sleeps a little and wakes with the light, a soft rain threading the place together. His hands are cold. As he moves, the sheep start to bleat and soon slither about in the crevice, scrambling on top of each other between him and Hemp.

Down Ard, on the other side of Knott Rigg, his feet are numb. 'Bloody boots,' he hears his father say. So he pounds a little harder, pushing into the constant thud, fern and moss shivering and cracking beneath. Pins and needles pushing day into his feet. He starts to canter down and as he raises his sights to Wandope, he feels his weight lift. All is simple, nothing but lifting to the peak, sheep bobbling behind, getting caught in gullies of too much bracken, catapulted out by Hemp down to Sail Beck.

And there, Stephen greets the beck with the pleasure of a loved one and drinks, splashing the cold chattering water onto his face, bellowing into his hands and calling up to the tributaries streaming down from the tops. To the calm around Sail sheltering the old cobalt mines where he sat with his father, flask in hand, quietly watching the North Western Fells change with the light. 'Come on, lad, up ye farrow.' It looks smooth. *Even the rains like to stay there a while,* he thinks. He would like to go up to Sail, but doesn't. His head hurts; a small rash stinging his cheek. He bathes it again and lies between the fells. The lower clouds move, bulging grey across a white sky. The curves of the valley cup him, though sometimes his belly feels weak, as if it drains with the water into the grass. He wonders if his mother is feeding the hens in the yard.

The lake is always a surprise. The edges are his, he could cut their shape into the ground with a knife. The water makes him stare; sinking in to find something. For a while it's still. The mountains bow deep into its bed and clouds sleep.

Hemp sits with him, mouth slightly open, his head flickers occasionally to one side of the lake, then the other. Some sheep have followed and are in a clearing, nibbling. Across the water, the sun lights up the banks of Mellbreak valley. It yellows the grass. Maybe Catherine will be up and folding sweet, creamy mixture into her black trays, her buckled hands clasping the spoon. He wonders what the hall feels like without him or his father there.

He digs into his bag, past packets of soup, tins of corned beef, sardines, and pulls out a box of cake. Vanilla sponge with gooseberry jam. The taste seems perfumed compared to the stillness of the view. Turning, he looks behind, as if the mountains would part to show the farm. And as he watches a lump rises in his chest and then pressure in his head before tears. He can hear the radio, listening to the races back by the hearth; him and his father with a bet on. He can see paperwork on the table, a mug of tea, the checked notebooks of annual bills and his schoolbooks, pages of homework done. His football cards sorted by the window: Moore, Charlton, Wilkins. The length of time feels weary. A coal-black cormorant takes flight, wings echoing. It pulls his sight back over Crummock Water and rests, tree like, on a small island. Sun slowly lights small green openings in the valley behind while the rest of the fells are in shade.

After some milk chocolate, he sets off along the water's edge and into the wood. Sheer streaks of slate crack into the lake. His headache affects his eye, makes the lid flicker. On the far side he moves past rushes and mallow ponds and through McKenzie's field, but soon becomes aware of the sound of Hemp growling.

'It'll be one lambing,' he says, as if his father were with him, and runs to find her on her side, belly swelling in and out like bellows to a fire.

He kneels near, not wanting to scare her, and watches as the milky sac balloons out and muddies. He can just see the lamb, white face, black eyes and dots of hooves. The sack sways. Hemp is lying low on the other side. Stephen calls him over.

'Ye daft mottle. Git 'ere.'

He holds his arm open for the dog to curl in and watch. But the sheep sees Hemp move and tries to bolt, scrambling to stand, her heaving belly falling back onto the head, bursting the sac. Stephen reaches forward, grabs the sheep and presses her to the ground, grating his leg on the gravel, leaning his knee on her leg, his hand on her head to stop her jolting.

'Down now, down.'

The sheep looks at him from the side with a wide, maddened eye and Stephen jerks with shock, shoulders hunched and he roars. The sound scares him, wakes him. His gut

191

sears with pain, spitting from the strain of holding the sheep. He grips it and roars again. His sound fills the space across the lake. Hemp is barking and Stephen looks up remembering the last time he saw his father alive, on the ledge of Wandope, curled for the night, cold. He remembers his father's eye, wide to the side and the way his father didn't know him, and the sounds he made, reluctant to be moved. No words, just sounds of disgust. He pulled his father's arm around his neck to help him up, but his broad body, heavy, slumped down, falling loose.

'Come on, Dad. We'll be having you home. We've all been out looking for you again.' But his father just wept, slapping his outspread legs with his knuckles, hands clenched in pain, head falling forward.

'Dad, it's me, Stephen. It'll be all right now. We've been looking for you. Just need to get you home. Come on now.' But his father scrambled only to kneel, head in hands, and shook sobbing to the ground, to the muddy slate and shingles, leaning into them. And then he began to bang, forehead thudding into the slate.

'Ey, no, now, Dad, no! Not that, Dad,' Stephen called as he pulled his father's broad shoulders, but the hitting got stronger and the murmurs of sobs became a rage and he roared. And then his father roared again and again as if he were vomiting sound until he pushed, and Stephen swung back to find him up and facing him, blooded brow dripping, shouting, ready to flatten him.

'Away ya devil, awe'eth ya, ya devil, I see you. Away,' staring from under his bunched brow, breathing heavily through his dripping nostrils like a bull.

'Dad, it's me.'

'Away, no, away now,' he grunted, staggering, blinking to the ground, fists poised for battle, head wet. Stephen stepped back, choking tears.

'Please, Dad, come home.'

'No, I'll not go home, no place for me,' he swayed. 'It'll be in these fells, or not at all. I'm not beaten yet.'

'Please let me help,' Stephen cried and the old man looked up to his son, wild, but recognising something of him for a moment.

'Get yourself away now, or I'll thrash you.' Fist clenched, body shaking he tumbled towards Stephen, 'I mean it, I'll thrash yer, get away, get away.' And Stephen ran, vision blurred, teared, to get help, leaving his father on the ledge, overhanging the sheer slate scree, heavy with night.

Breathless, Stephen focuses on the edge of the lake, the grass and then the sheep. 'Come on now!' he whispers out of breath and lets his weeping head fall forward onto the fleece while he reaches over and slips his hand around and under the back of the lamb's head to pull it out. The sticky sac covering his skin, warm water down his arm. He moves round and pulls, mindful of the suction, the sheep kicking while the lamb's head slides out and rests; complete in itself, white and asleep. Then the body, yellow wool swaddled in glutinous white.

Thighs holding the sheep, Stephen scrapes his finger into the lamb's mouth, scrubs its nostrils with grass and gathers it into both hands, bringing its limp body, in as much sac as possible, over to the mother's face. He lies behind her, holding her in, his chest on the mother's back, his blood blotting her wool, carefully bending her towards the lamb, to the smell.

'Come on, mother,' he whispers, loud but gently. 'Come on there now,' and he holds her till he feels her licking, while the twists of umbilical cord slither out with the placenta, and he gently rolls away, leaving them together. The lamb waking, shuddering its head, soon splaying its hooves, ready to stand and dart at the mother's underbelly, tail wiggling.

Over the far side of Crummock Water Stephen's mind refuses the presence of Red Pike, pushing the purple grey, as if there were lakes on either side of him. When he gets to Blea Crag the light changes and his steps quicken towards Mellbreak as the valley opens between them. Pools of sun circle a log or bank as if it's held. The bark of a tree is warmed to the side so that it leans in peace.

By afternoon, clouds have covered the skies, to part again in the nook between the twin fells. Veins of bronze lengthen into straight, certain lines, reminding the valley it is marked. Stephen rests by the tall juniper, a silver birch partly entwined. He throws a large stick into the lake and watches Hemp's white nose and black ears bob after it. His arm begins to cramp so he walks the valley, luscious in its meadow mint, dandelions, forget-me-nots, speedwells and buttercups; their colours pulling him this way and that, catching the sun.

For a moment his sight is drawn towards Haystacks in the distance where dark streaks pull over the lake. Rain is making a stake in the ground. It comes in fast hissing at the waters, stickling the waves to break in on each other. He makes a cover with some tarpaulin under the branches of the juniper tree and pulls Hemp by his collar onto his lap; his long fur is soaked. The sky cracks, thunder races along the ground and heavy, purple clouds hammer. It rains as if it only rains.

And then the clouds move on, fast, black tumbling over grey, rolling into the fells. Light soon blinking in, widening to whiten the water. Mist so still, it absorbs him and the valley. *A good place to rest*, he thinks. The haze thickens to pearl before sunset sieves through, unwrapping the mountains in gold, and he feels his father there. Remembers the weight of him as they leant against the tree. Tenderness burrows into his heart like a fist. Dust around him lifts in the heat like smoke from fire, incense into clear skies. His father was almost lashed when he found him. Bloodied chest. He leans out towards the lake, hovering, fragile over the waters. Sadness seeps out of him like spring rain.

He recovers as if he has been in a sleep and feels uneasy. Something bothers him in the back of his mind. So, he walks, clearing the grasses of last year's twigs and old wood. He pulls out bracken bent and frayed, black rotten roots, dragging the gnarled branches left to moss and crumble. He isn't sure why he's gathering old lint, just bends, clawing the reeds, jaggeding the gorse with scoured hands, freeing thorned bushel. He works when he is out of breath. He works as dusk fades with the taste of lemon into burnt-yellow. And keeps working, back wet with sweat, as the mountains are neon, back-lit, like peering through a door.

As darkness settles and the chill of clear sky pricks his skin, he uses kerosene from the camper stove and lights the mound of fire blazing east into the night. Silt and smoke race in tar black. Sap spits and tinder sparks snap, hot tendered, stoked through the hours till the fire's embers join with the dawn. And there, covered in ash, he is finally worn and heavy enough to sleep. He kneels, sore eyed; a quick glance up Mellbreak valley and sees something moving; a man, maybe someone he knows. *Too bright at first, but in time he's clearer, a stranger walking down through the valley towards him, the spring of cowslip, yarrow and heather beneath his feet. Meadowsweet morning seeping through the grasses, lifting their heads, marrying cotton-soft smoke. Stephen's so tired he can hardly watch but the light draws him in. The man is far away though somehow he can see his black leather boots knotted to the sides, a hurrumph on the grass, fallowed green tweed in his cap. A farmer's cap; watching his sheep laid out in the fields, rest in his skin, warm wool breathing.*

The man stops at a tarn, searching through the bladderwort, the curled yellows hanging like bells over matted weave. Reeds lean to the side content by a tombstone: a young man taken by gas. But the waters don't rest there in the valley, no, a small stream cuckoles on rounded rocks, splitheres at overhangs running to the waters beyond. And the man knows that as he walks.

Seeds in his pocket. Stephen knows there are seeds in his pocket and buckled crab apples. An old handkerchief to offer, stitched trim round the hem. Broad thumbs grained with soil. He smiles a narrow slice, an uneven mouth like cracked bark. And his eyes, his brown eyes are like chestnuts in winter steaming.

196

Near the lake he stands by the juniper tree, its nest of branches raised, a silver birch sewn into its roots. The man is beyond familiar. If Stephen coughed he would break into sobs. And as the man stands there, Stephen's gaze open, autumn draws in, splitting the soil, loosening the grasses. Tall stems honey and stoop. Silver birch leaves yellow and fall, scuffled against the trunk. Freckled fronds rust; they would crack.

An easy lift to climb the tree, Stephen's breath rising as the man's feet hook into the rope-veined trunk, his grey jacket snared in twigs, ankles scraped. Netted, he stretches through the thicket, scouring his wrists and stands, arms spread, looking out across the lake. His strained belly breathes hard, pressed in, shirt lifted. His skin is hopeful in rain, wet cheek resting against a branch. Frost in his tears.

And now, as snow begins, the man sucks air deep into his belly. A widening of breath. A vision so close to Stephen, it's his breath, his cheek. He closes his eyes and leans forward to fall, weight pulling him through the thicket. Scuffle and thwack scours his face, caught in shudders of brisk and stem. One arm tunnelled through, the other held back, jacket ripped, broken spindles pulling sleeve and collar, his shoulder falling. The bloodied shirt, once washed at home and buttoned over yellowed vest, ironed.

A thunderous snap releases him further, open ribbed, half hanging, half caught by a hard front branch while snow, dishevelled in its veiling, disorders the sky.

Here the water comes, thurrowing from the lake, willowing through the rocks, filling the soil. It moves like mud, seeping through roots of broken bracken, bending the heads of mudwort, the tired vetch and clover, the brittle open

butterwort, the saxifrage and campion, pulling, pulling, con-
suming them with the tide. It seals the valley; lapping the
juniper, the dark brittle juniper. Mirroring it in shivers of
wind.

The water's high now, silver in evening calm. A falling
branch drops, plomp. It echoes across the lake but the sur-
face hardly moves. It seeps over the branch like oil. His feet
are bare and childlike, the severed roots of branches through
his palms. He dangles, coughing through streaked teeth, red
drops on water and the lake lifts, a dark bulb of mercury.
It swells, edgeless, belly-black, drawing him in. It would stick.

Ah, his eyes close, arms given in slump. His skin is paper
thin. It dries like salted parchment and catches against the
bark; mouth drooped to the side. In rain he would slip and
stretch to gaping holes. His breath is long and throaty. It
rumbles then stops, chest bumping, before he breathes again.
He is given. He is gift, devoured, lifting his heavy chin, to
squint over the water's rim. It watches without iris. Waiting,
stone cold and empty. He could fall. His hands are pierced
and empty.

A crack, a shudder and the juniper's bark sprays like pow-
dered thunder onto the water. It grates the salts from his skin
and tangles down. It thumps the water's rim with wooded
sinews and leaks its sap. It drums the lake, it pierces the
water and the man's eyes fix beneath his brow with a snap.
A wry smile. His dry body would drink.

And look how the water goes, slow at first, loosening its
wine. Look how it draws back, like wind, alive, pulling lines
of sedge and fescue, sweeping tangled sward. And up in the
branches, the new copper branches, not yet swathed with

threaded grey, his hands lump into soft bud, leaves unfurl, their wax-green cupping berries of velvet milk. See the gold streaking through clouds, frizzing the grasses, twitching the stems. Lichen uncurls into leather lace on stone, moss furs, ferns spiral tight.

And there, a flock of starlings burst above the tree, a slice to the flutter of wings. Swarming above the lake, they turn into a dart, a steep surrender. Hands in flight.

The Countess of Mar: My Lords, I am grateful to the noble Lord for that reply. Is he aware that it is some 13 years since I started asking questions about organophosphates? ... can he explain if organophosphates are safe and, if they have been tested for their safety, efficacy, and their quality, why farmers have been required since that time to wear space suits when they are dipping and to have a proficiency certificate to allow them to buy sheep dips? Why are all those precautions taken if they are safe?

The Ecologist 28 March 2012

Developed as a nerve gas before the 2nd World War, OPs were being championed in 1951 as an insecticide for killing bugs and pests that damaged livestock and crops. Lord Zuckerman, later to be the government's chief scientist, warned of the dangers of allowing farmers to use the newly emerging organophosphate pesticides (OPs). He stated that chemicals could be absorbed through the skin or inhalation and, as such, farmers should receive detailed instructions on protecting themselves and that all containers should be clearly labelled as 'deadly poison'. It wouldn't be until the 1990s that this last recommendation was finally implemented.

World Health Organization, United Nations

Initial Summary of the Main Factors Contributing to Incidents of Acute Pesticide Poisoning 6 June 2002 Misa Kishi, MD, DrPH

OVERVIEW OF FINDINGS

Cholinesterase-inhibiting pesticides (i.e. organophosphates and carbamates) have been identified as the most common causes of severe acute pesticide poisonings, some of which have resulted in deaths.

Acknowledgements

In gratitude to:
Damien Doorley, Barbara Turner Vesselago,
David Hunter, Rowan Routh, Andrew Humphries,
Poppy Hampson, Jenny Hewson, Peter Straus, Philip
Langeskov, Giles Foden, Sian Wheldon, Dr William
Rollinson, SOAS Missionary Archives, the Hayton,
Smallwood, Cockburn and Mars families, and
Great Aunt Margaret Miller.

MELLBREAK : Dawn breaking on a fell
(local Cumbrian translation)

MELL : Dawn
(local Cumbrian translation)

MELL : Short passage which leads to the fire house
(The Cumbrian Dictionary of Dialect, Tradition
and Folklore - William Rollinson 1997)

MELINO : Yellow
(Celtic Lexicon, University of Wales, 2016)

MELTA : Lightning
(Celtic Lexicon, University of Wales, 2016)

BREAK : The portion of land ploughed out of grass
(The Cumbrian Dictionary of Dialect, Tradition
and Folklore - William Rollinson 1997)

BREK : The portion of land ploughed out of grass
(Comprehensive Dictionary of Cumberland
Dialect - William Dickinson, 1859 ed.
Richard M. Byers 2006)

BREKKA : Hill slope
(English-Old Norse Dictionary Compiled by
Ross G. Arthur 2002)

BRIG : Mountain
(Celtic Lexicon, University of Wales, 2016)

penguin.co.uk/vintage